"This is a book you won't be able to put down. Ida keeps you asking, 'What's going to happen next?' *Anticipated* is an age-old story told from a different perspective. You will understand more of the Jewish culture and how astounding the life of Christ was. How his life affected and still affects us all."
—**Misty Clark,** author of the always entertaining blog: "Moms for Lowered Expectations."

"*Anticipated* is a wonderful story about the Jewish response to Jesus the Messiah in the first century A.D. The author's description of Jesus is based upon solid research and a realistic portrayal of the different responses to Jesus by first century Jews, as seen through the eyes of Bethlehem shepherd boy Uzziel. Uzziel grows into manhood, expecting a fierce warrior-Messiah who would lead an army to oust the Romans from Israel. The adult Jesus is very, very different from what Uzziel and his fellow Jews had originally expected. Uzziel's reaction to Jesus forms the core of the story, as Uzziel works to reshape his expectations. Jesus the infant, Jesus the toddler at the time of King Herod's attempt to kill him, and Jesus the teacher in circa 30 A.D. are all based upon the probable realities that Jesus and his detractors, as well as his followers faced, rather than upon a fantasy version of what Jesus, Mary, and Joseph should have been like in too many less well-researched writers' minds.

I came away from the novel with a clearer understanding of why many first century Jews rejected Jesus and his teachings, as well as why some Jews came around to understanding the real reason why Jesus the Messiah came to earth. Not only was the novel fun reading, but also very informative. The grammar is flawless, making for easy reading and an ample desire to keep turning the pages. Author Ida Smith knows her craft.
—**Paul F. Murray,** Readers' Favorite

ANTICIPATED

IDA SMITH

Harley,
I'm glad you were able
to attend the conference and
wish you the best as
you write.
God Bless.
Ida Smith

A JAGGED JOURNEYS' NOVELLA

ANTICIPATED
BY IDA SMITH

To learn more about Jagged Journeys' Stories or sign up to receive free short stories, visit: http://idasmithbooks.com

ISBN-13: 978-0-9976530-0-7
ISBN-10: 0997653007

FICTION / CHRISTIAN / HISTORICAL

This book is a work of historical fiction based on biblical events. Any person, place, or incident not taken directly from scripture is purely a product of the author's imagination.

Scripture quotations are from the Holy Bible, New International Version, copyright © 1973, 1978, 1984, and 2011 by International Bible Society.

Ida can be contacted by mail at: P.O. Box 2237, Lewiston, ID 83501 or email at: stories@idasmithbooks.com

Set in Times New Roman
Printed in the United States of America

To Virginia Patterson

Thank you for your love, steadfastness, consistency, and strength of character. You have been a true role model and the best mother I could ever want. I am blessed to have you as both my mother and my friend.

PROLOGUE

Anticipation—nothing is ever exactly as we expect. That is how it was with his arrival.

With every passing day, we anticipated his coming. It would be soon. We all knew it. It had to be. How could he allow this injustice to continue?

The promise of his coming lingered for years. But now—now was his time. We were certain. It was in our thoughts, spoken of behind closed doors, woven between whispers as our oppressors marched by. As they taxed our meager wages and issued their decrees. We longed for his appearing as that usurper set himself up as *our* king.

We anticipated his arrival all our lives, yet when he came, we were completely unprepared. It didn't matter that there were over three hundred prophesies—most of which we'd memorized. Somehow, between the distance of those prophesies and the desperation of our situation—we twisted their meaning. A fact we wouldn't understand for decades. A reality some never accepted.

My name is Uzziel. I saw him the night of his arrival—and when they raised him up as our king—anticipation altered beyond recognition. This is my story.

THE GIFT

CHAPTER ONE

UNEXPECTED VISITORS

I cinched my cloak tighter against the night air, angry that Shai and I had to sleep on the roof. As if it wasn't enough that strangers slept on our mats in the house, all around us the noise of so many people in our small village made sleep difficult—at least for me.

Above me, the Maker's cloak darkened the sky—only the light of his presence sparkled through the weave to shine upon us. This beauty was my only solace amidst the ruckus we'd experienced for the past several weeks—thanks to Caesar Augustus and his people-counting officials. Let them count us—as if the stars could be counted. The Romans might control the ground we trod on, but for all their power and might they couldn't control the skies.

Despite the cool night I smiled at this thought. That's when I saw it. A star—so bright and big I knew I'd never seen it before.

I nudged Shai. "Look, look at that star."

He grumbled something and rolled over to peer up.

"What do you think it means?"

"That it's time to go to sleep," my cousin mumbled.

"Shai, I'm serious. I think it means something. Don't you remember what Rabbi Harel said?"

"Rabbi Harel says lots of things. Now go to sleep."

"Remember the scriptures we copied a while ago? That when Yahweh put the lights in the sky they were to serve as signs to mark

3

sacred times, days and years?"

He grunted.

"Or what about the prophet Isaiah?"

"What about him? Come on, Uzziel, it's late and tomorrow we have chores, and lessons, and—"

"The people walking in darkness have seen a great light—"

"I wouldn't call that a great light."

"It's brighter than all the others," I countered.

"How do you remember all this stuff, anyway?"

"How do you not? Don't you want to be a Rabbi?"

"Of course I do. Doesn't every boy in Israel? But right now, I'm going to sleep." Shai rolled over and quit talking.

I stared up at the star, shimmering to the east of us, larger and closer than the others. Shai had fallen asleep, his annoying wheeze filled the air until footsteps and whispers down the street overtook his wheezing. I crawled to the low wall and peered over into the narrow street. I expected to see Roman soldiers. Oh, how I wanted to pelt one with a rock. My fingers caressed the slingshot and bag of smooth stones by my side. Shai mocked me for sleeping with them, but I protested that we must always be prepared.

But if I hit one, and I was a pretty good aim, I would probably be caught. And even if I weren't, some other person would be accused and punished; punished far more severely than the crime deserved. I shuddered at the thought and pushed that incident out of my mind. Besides, that was several years ago, when I was only nine. What could I have done to save the accused?

The sounds below diverted my thoughts. To my surprise the men in the street weren't soldiers, they weren't even Romans. I watched as they hurried toward our home.

"Why are we going this way?" one of them said.

"It's faster than going around."

I cocked my head. I could swear that was my uncle Roi's voice.

The men passed our home and headed up the street. I saw my uncle's tall slender frame, a hand's breadth above the others. How odd. Why was he in town?

I slipped down the stairs that led to the alley and followed them. I'd walked several blocks when I heard other footsteps and turned to see a pair of Roman guards round a corner onto the road. My uncle and the others turned left and I slipped into a doorway, hidden by the darkness.

I held my breath as the soldiers approached. I didn't want to explain why I was lurking about, not to them or my father. The soldiers were now beside my hiding spot. I stared into the eyes of a short burley Roman.

My hands chilled and my heart rattled in my chest. No matter what I'd say, the guards would think I was looking to steal something from some of the many travelers in town for the census.

I froze. What would I tell my father?

"Ahem," the guard cleared his throat.

I almost fell to my knees to beg mercy. But the guard turned his head and kept walking.

My arms and shoulders fell limp and I gasped for air. I peered around the doorway in time to see the guards wander down the street. I crept across the road into an alley, waited for a few moments and slunk to another doorway.

The soldiers stopped. The burley one turned around.

I pressed my body as flat as I could against the wall.

"What is it?" the other asked.

"I thought I heard something. Footsteps."

Pebbles and sand crushed between the cobblestone and the soldier's sandals as he approached. He was now only a few feet away. Why had I left my hiding spot so soon?

"Come on, Antonius. It was probably just a dog."

The approaching soldier grunted. "Yeah, a Jewish dog."

I touched the small pouch that held my stones but remained hidden. The guards continued down the road. I watched until they were out of sight then moved to the corner where my uncle and the others had disappeared.

I started down the passage, lit only by the moon and stars. I passed an inn where people slept on tables and benches. Up ahead, I saw the men leaving our village. I glanced behind me and saw no one so I proceeded down the road.

Up ahead was Migdal Eder, the tower of the flock. A door opened and light silhouetted my uncle and the other men. They entered and the light disappeared behind the shut door. Above, the bright star hovered to my right, just behind the tower.

I scurried to catch up to them. Around me, I occasionally heard the rustle or bleat of sheep scattered in the fields. I hid in the tower's shadow. The Levitical shepherds used the tower of the flock to watch the temple sheep and birth the sacrificial lambs. What could my uncle and these men be doing here in the middle of the night? I strained to hear voices while I waited.

It seemed as though the men were staying and I considered going home when the door opened and light spilled out along with the men. I pressed my body to the cool stones.

"It was just as we were told," a man said.

"And the fulfillment of Micah's words," my uncle Roi said.

"He is perfect," said another.

"Of course he is," replied Uncle Roi.

"Did you see him, wrapped in cloths like a sacrificial lamb?"

"Lying in the manger just like we lay the lambs."

"You noticed that too?" said my uncle.

"Yes," several answered and nodded in agreement.

"What could it mean?"

There was a murmuring as they each voiced their perplexity.

"Look at me." One of the men pulled up his sleeve. "I have goose flesh."

"Did you see the way he looked at us?" another asked.

"It was as if he knew me."

"Shush, keep your voices down," my uncle warned.

"It's all so unreal."

"But it is real," Uncle Roi said.

"I've got to tell my family."

"Me too."

"Go and tell your family and friends," my uncle said. "Then we must get back to our sheep."

With that, the men dispersed. I watched until they entered the village. Alone, I stepped onto the road.

What had they seen? I inched my way to the door, a sliver of light from a lamp within escaped around the edges. I wanted just a peek. I pried the door just a little. *Creak.* I sensed movement on the other side. Before I could turn and run, the door opened. A man looked down at me, his face chiseled with light and shadow. I stepped back, unsure what to do or say.

"Do you want to see him too?"

I stared into his face, unable to speak.

He beckoned me in.

I entered, wondering the whole time what enticed the temple shepherds to leave the sacred lambs in the fields and come to these stalls. Lambing season was still several months away. My vision adjusted in the light.

The lambing room was clean and unpopulated. There, in one of the stalls, knelt a young woman over a manger hewn from stone.

"Go." The man motioned me forward.

Something in the manger moved. I stepped closer and saw an infant, his body wrapped in strips of old, soft cloth—the cloth used to calm and protect the lambs so they would remain perfect for sacrifice. I looked at the young mother, her face soft, smiling as she caressed the child's cheek.

"Come," she said.

I approached and knelt down by the child. "What is his name?"

"Joshua ben Joseph."

The baby looked at me. I reached out my finger and touched his tiny hand. He wrapped his slender fingers around mine.

"Why were the shepherds here?"

"To see him."

"Why?"

"They said angels told them to come," the mother said.

"Angels?"

She nodded and I could see a mixture of excitement and awe on her face.

Who was this child that angels would tell of his birth? My mind reeled with questions.

Her husband bent and looked down at his son. "Why did you come?"

"I—I—I saw the shepherds and followed them."

He smiled.

The shepherds. My uncle. He would be going home to tell my father. "I need to go."

They looked at me with surprise. "So soon?"

"My parents don't know I'm gone."

"Oh," they said.

"I'm glad you came," the mother said.

I nodded. Not sure what this was all about, I slipped onto the road then sprinted for home. Upon entering the village I looked for soldiers. Light from oil lamps flickered behind lattice and between cracks in shutters throughout my village. I passed homes and heard hushed whispers. I was eager to get home and learn what this was all about.

Halfway there I heard footsteps behind me and turned.

"Boy, what are you doing out at this time of night?"

I froze.

"Boy, I'm talking to you."

"Yes, sir."

"Well?"

I looked up into the face of a young soldier. He couldn't have been more than ten years older than me. "I—I—I couldn't sleep."

The guard folded his muscular arms across his broad chest. "Really? So you thought you'd just go for a walk?"

"I thought it might make me tired."

He narrowed his eyes then glanced around. "What's going on? Why are so many people up? He pointed down a side street where a door stood ajar revealing light from within.

"I don't know."

He shoved me up against a stone wall. "I think you do."

"Honestly, I don't know."

"Where did you go on this little walk of yours?"

Anger swelled inside me. What business was it of his where I went? This was our country, not the Romans'. I glanced at the dagger and sword attached to his belt.

"Answer me."

"I just walked around."

He leaned in closer. "I don't think you're telling me everything— boy. What's your name?"

"Uzziel."

He eyed me closely. "What is your father's name?"

"Maor."

"What does he do?"

"He sells cloth that our family weaves, sir."

The young soldier thought for a moment. "I know who he is."

I waited in silence, not knowing how to respond. I hoped he

wouldn't take me to my father.

"Why are so many people awake at this hour?"

"I don't know," I said.

"I think trouble is soldering."

"Trouble, sir?"

"Trouble." Light from an opened door flashed across his hard eyes and scowling face. "And you're going to find out and tell me."

A lump filled my throat. If there was trouble, why would I want to tell him, of all people?

"You find out and come to the barracks, tomorrow, after your lessons. Ask for Magnus. You understand?"

"Yes, sir."

He leaned in; his rank breath stung my nostrils and eyes. "And if you don't come, I'll come looking for you."

I nodded.

"Now get home." He gave me one last shove into the wall then let go of me.

I ran home, sensing his steel eyes burning into my back.

CHAPTER TWO

STRANGE NEWS

I slipped into our home. The lamps were lit and everyone, including my younger siblings and our guests were up.

"Uzziel, where have you been?" my mother, Sarah, asked, my baby brother, Maayan, in her arms. "Your Uncle Roi has something important he wants to tell us." Before I could answer she ordered me to help my sister with Orel. I moved to where Kelila sat with Orel fidgeting on her small lap. I lifted my little brother into my arms.

I looked at my Uncle Roi who half sat, half squatted like I'd seen him do so often in the fields. All around him, family and guests sat or stood. My uncle gave me a knowing look, as though we shared a secret.

"Quiet everyone," my father said. The gray in his dark hair added to the sense of authority he naturally commanded. "My family and our honored guests: tonight is a very important night for Israel. The time we have so long awaited has arrived."

The men sat up straighter at these words and several women gasped. Others pressed fingers to their lips.

My uncle leaned on his staff as he looked at us then spoke. "Those of you who are guests in our home, my name is Roi. I am a descendant of Levi and I tend to the temple sheep."

Several of our guests nodded.

Uncle Roi continued, "Tonight, as we sat around the fire I sensed we were being watched. The ram at my feet trembled. I looked up, expecting to see the fire's reflection in the eyes of a wolf or lion. Instead, a tall broad-shouldered man approached. A bright, warm light emanated from him and though he had feet, he hovered above the ground. He was dressed in shimmering white with a large sword by his side. His arms and legs were strong and when he spoke his voice was mighty and commanding."

"Were you scared father? Were you scared?" Hadar asked, her eyes wide.

"Oh, yes. We all shook and fell to our knees, afraid he would slay us. Afraid with a fear different than any we'd experienced in fighting off thieves or wild animals."

"Oh, my," Bashe, Roi's wife said. She was pale, her fingers pressed against her protruding belly. "Was he an angel?"

"Yes." Uncle Roi's face was solemn. "We knew that this was no ordinary man, but a heavenly being."

The room erupted with questions and comments.

One of our guests stood. "I know I am just a guest in this home," the man said, his wife and three children near him. "But are we to believe that an angel came and spoke to you, a mere shepherd?"

"Not just me, but all of us out there in the field tonight."

"I think this is just a story you've made up to impress or entertain us and keep us from our sleep."

Kelila rolled her eyes at me. "He thinks he's better than us because he lives in Jerusalem."

My father stood, his hands held out. "Quiet, quiet. I know this sounds—" he glanced at Uncle Roi, "fanciful. But I tell you, my brother is an honest man. Let's hear him out."

"Humph," our guest said and crossed his arms.

Uncle Roi looked at the man with disgust then continued. "We bowed before him in reverent fear our hearts pounding in our chests. 'Do not be afraid,' he said, his voice commanding yet calm. 'I bring you good news of great joy for all people. Today, in the town of David a Savior has been born to you; he is the Messiah, the Lord.' "

Silence filled our home as my uncle's words sunk into our minds and hearts like a long anticipated rain on parched soil. How many, many years had our people waited for this moment? How many centuries had our people looked forward to the fulfillment of ancient prophesies? Even now, as the town around us swelled with people brought here by Caesar Augustus' census, the fulfillment of our Savior's arrival was in our hearts, and on our tongues, and minds. I thought of the infant I'd seen less than an hour ago. The parents didn't seem surprised that I had come. Did they know?

"The Messiah? The promised Messiah? He's here?" asked a guest.

A wide smile spread across Uncle Roi's lips. "Yes."

Then, everyone spoke; first in halting whispers then boldly.

"A Savior has been born?" asked another guest.

"Yes." My uncle nodded. "He is the Messiah, the Lord. The Savior we've all been waiting for. The angel told us we would, 'find a baby wrapped in cloths and lying in a manger.' "

"So, did you?" Our contentious guest asked.

I despised this man. He was as bad as any Roman.

Uncle Roi raised his hand as if to tell this man to be patient. "I realized then," he continued, "that the angel expected us to go and find this child. The very thought spread excitement through my every muscle."

We all quieted, our attention focused on my uncle.

"Then—" Uncle Roi stood, his arms outstretched above us, "the sky was full of angels."

"Angels," several small children repeated.

"To my right and to my left. Before us and behind us. Angels—brighter than the noonday sun. Beautiful, powerful beings, taller than any human, their arms as strong as branches and their legs like pillars. Their chests were the width of two men and each wore a sword by his side. They sang with voices clear and clean like mountain water."

"What did they say?" Asked Shai's mother.

Uncle Roi's smile spread wide across his face. "In unison, they praised God, singing, 'Glory to God in the highest heaven, and on earth peace to those on whom his favor rests.' "

At his words I caught my breath. "A whole host of angels?"

My uncle nodded and I looked at Kelila with five-year-old Orel back on her lap. Their eyes were wide as were the other children's. This was the stuff of ancient stories.

"Their singing was the most beautiful sound I'd ever heard. We all just peered up at them in awe. Then, as quickly as they appeared, they were gone."

"Where'd they go, Papa?"

Uncle Roi smiled down at Hadar and shrugged his shoulders. "I don't know my little desert flower. I guess they went back to heaven." He looked out at the rest of us. "We shepherds sat in silence, the fire's light dim against the surrounding darkness. The angels' words, their voices, their very presence filled us with warmth until we could sit no longer."

"So you came to town to look for him, right Uncle Roi?"

"Yes, Uzziel. We left several to watch the sheep, promising they could come as soon as we returned, then hurried to town."

"And you found him?" My father asked.

"Yes, lying in a manger, wrapped in strips of cloth."

An excitement grew within me. Was the child I saw really the promised Messiah? I remembered the strips of old cloth wrapped around his tiny body to warm him and protect his internal organs. Someday he would need real clothing. I thought about the piece of warm wool on my loom.

"The promised Messiah, lying in a manger?" Our contentious guest shook his head in disbelief. "Why would Yahweh allow His promised king to arrive in a place where sheep are born? And why in such a tiny town?"

"But doesn't the prophet say that out of Bethlehem will come one who will be ruler over Israel, even though we are small?" The words burst from my mouth before I realized I'd said them.

The guest and my father both glared at me but Uncle Roi grinned. "You have been learning your lessons well, Uzziel."

ಐ ◆ ಲ

We spoke in hushed tones as to what this all meant for us and for our nation. As children whimpered, mothers hustled us off to bed, the smaller children already asleep in their arms. Uncle Roi left for the fields and Shai and I returned to the roof.

"Where were you?" Shai asked. "Your mother and father were getting concerned."

I couldn't help grinning. "I saw him."

"Who?"

"The Messiah."

"What? How?"

"I heard Uncle Roi and the shepherds and followed them."

Shai shook his head. "Uzziel, you take too many chances."

"How did I know where they were going? I just thought it was strange they weren't in the field."

"Do you really think that the Messiah was born, here, in Bethlehem?"

"Yes. The prophets said he'd be born here. But why in a shepherd's watchtower?" I stood and looked north at Migdal Eder. "He's the Messiah. He should have been born—" I turned and looked to the southeast to the Herodium. "He should have been born in a palace."

"Yahweh can do what he wants. Did our ancestors expect Him to feed them with the bread of angels in the desert? Did anyone expect a shepherd boy to kill a giant-sized soldier. Maybe Yahweh likes to surprise us."

"I know, but why a baby? Do you know how long we're going to have to wait until he overthrows the Romans?"

"Every man must first be born a baby," Shai said, always enjoying to point out the obvious. "I'm sure Yahweh's got the timing all worked out."

"Shai, you are so infuriating. Doesn't it bother you that the Romans rule over us?"

"Of course, but if this baby is the Messiah, what can we do?"

I looked up at the bright star. "I know." I lay down next to him and lowered my voice. "We can raise an army and make him king when he's our age. Josiah became king when he was eight years old. Why not the Messiah?"

Shai looked at me. "I know you don't like the Romans."

"Don't like?"

"Alright, hate. But raise an army? Uzziel, are you kidding me? The Romans will discover you and you'll just get yourself killed. Honestly, Uzziel. Besides, remember the angels' message?"

I looked at him.

" 'Glory to God in the highest heaven, and on earth peace to those on whom his favor rests.' Peace Uzziel, not war." With that, Shai rolled over and I soon heard his wheezy snore.

Shai was just too conformist. He didn't like change and especially didn't like danger or risk. He didn't realize the opportunity God had given us. Here was the promised Messiah. We owed him our allegiance. I knew if I thought about it long enough I could figure out a way to raise and train an army without the Romans finding out.

The Romans—Magnus. What was I going to do about him? I needed to keep Magnus, and the other soldiers for that matter away from our future king.

CHAPTER THREE

KEEPING A SECRET

"**N**ow boys," Rabbi Harel paced back and forth in front of us. "There are rumors circulating that the promised Messiah was born here, in Bethlehem, last night."

Whispers seeped out like wine from a cracked jug.

He stopped and looked directly at us. We quieted.

"I know we are all eager to be liberated from the Romans. But we must be careful about such things. We mustn't jump to any hasty conclusions. To do such could be dangerous for all our people."

Danger. Boy was he right. The Messiah had been here less than a day and already I had a zealot Roman soldier demanding information from me. Part of me wanted to say, *What happened last night? Oh, just the birth of our promised Messiah who's going to run you rotten Romans out of Israel. Other than that, not much.* I smiled at the thought.

"How can we know if this baby is the promised Messiah?" asked one of the boys.

"What do the prophets say of such things?" Rabbi Harel asked, now drilling us on the Messianic prophecies.

What if I told Magnus I couldn't find anything out? Yet the whole village was whispering behind covered lips about the birth. If I made something up he would be sure to discover it was a lie. Why did I have to follow Uncle Roi? If I hadn't then I wouldn't be in this mess. But, I also wouldn't have seen our future King. I smiled knowing of all my friends I was the only one who'd seen him.

Still mulling over my options, I half listened to our teacher as he spoke five words from the sacred texts then called to various students to finish the passages. When we were dismissed all of us boys gathered about swapping snippets of information. "Our uncle was there," Shai boasted.

"Your uncle saw the promised Messiah?" several asked.

"So did Uzziel," Shai said.

"Shush." I glared at Shai and then the others all staring at me with expectant looks. "We must be careful. What do you think the Romans will do if they find out?" I ran my fingers across my neck. "We must do our best to protect him."

"Uzziel here wants to raise an army to make him king."

A few of the more timid boys faded into the background and slipped home. "Yeah, let's do that," several said.

"We're too young," two or three argued.

"Not right now," I said. "Right now we just need to keep the Romans from finding out about him."

They nodded.

"Then we'll start training—though we'll say we're just playing or training to fight lions and thieves."

"Yeah, great idea."

"We'll talk later."

The boys nodded, some hesitantly I noticed and we went our separate ways.

"The promised Messiah. Uzziel, can you believe he's here? In our town? In our lifetime?" Shai was finally excited. It took Rabbi Harel and the other boys in our class to wake him from his stupor.

"That's what Uncle Roi and I have been trying to tell you."

"I know, but Rabbi Harel said, 'But you, Bethlehem Ephrathah, though you are small among the clans of Judah—' "

" '—out of you will come for me one who will be ruler over Israel, whose origins are from of old, from days of eternity.' " I finished, trying to direct the path we took.

"Uzziel, why are you going the long way home?" Shai asked as I started up the hill.

"Why not?"

"But the way past the barracks is faster."

I knew I had to go by the barracks and tell Magnus and explain to him what the "trouble" was. Maybe I could tell him I had to do an errand for my father. "Um, there's something I want to see this way."

"What?"

"Uh, if Lior needs more cloth."

Shai cocked his head at me. "Since when are you concerned about selling cloth?"

"Well, I was thinking, if I don't become a Rabbi I'll eventually take over the family business. If that happens, I'd better become familiar with our customers and let them know they can trust me."

Shai raised an eyebrow. "So are you going to sell cloth by day and fight the Romans at night?"

"Shush," I glanced around to see who might have heard him. "I can do both."

"Sure you can."

I glared at my ever-practical cousin.

Half way up the hill, Magnus stepped out from a potter's shop. "Uzziel, son of Maor. I thought you might be coming this way."

"Uh, you did?"

He crossed his muscular arms across his broad chest. "Why don't you tell your cousin here to go on home."

I gulped. Was it possible this dumb Roman knew more than I thought? "Go on home, Shai, I'll be there soon."

Shai's face paled and his upper lip twitched. "All—alright."

"Don't tell anyone," I whispered.

He nodded.

Magnus' shadow shrouded me from the afternoon sun. "Did you forget we had an appointment?"

"No, sir. I was just running an errand for the family business."

His cheek extended as he pressed his tongue against it. "So, what was all the commotion about last night?"

I took a deep breath. "Well, I'm not sure." I tried to force the fear from my voice. "From what I can tell, a family of travelers arrived late last night. But, with all the people in town for the census, they couldn't find a place to sleep."

"People have been arriving regularly since the decree without all the ruckus of last night," the soldier countered. "There's more to last night's affairs than a family looking for lodging. There have been murmurings all day about some child."

Oh no! What all did he know? What did the other soldiers know? I gulped. Child. Child. What could I say about a child? "Well, sir. Apparently, while this family attempted to find a place to sleep one of the children wandered off. So people were searching for the child."

Magnus spit near my feet. "A lost child?"

"Uh huh." I was so nervous my innards shook. What would he do if he learned I had lied? I couldn't allow myself to think about all the ways he could hurt me. I consoled myself with the fact it wasn't a complete lie. The shepherds were looking for a child. And they did go and tell everyone else about the child. So, yes, that was as close to the truth as this Roman heathen needed. "Yep, a child. All that ruckus last night was about finding a child."

"You're not lying to me, are you?"

I shook my head. Afraid if I spoke I'd give myself away.

"If I learn you've lied to me I'll have you whipped. You under-stand?"

I nodded.

He looked around at the people and animals that passed us on the narrow street.

It looked as though he believed my story. Why hadn't I thought of this earlier? Soon I would be freed of him and could—.

"Did they find it?"

His words jolted me back to the present. "Find what?"

"The child."

"Oh, yes. They did. I guess the child was tired and wandered into a stable and fell asleep in a manger."

"Stupid people. How can we count them if they keep getting lost?"

I shrugged, but he was already shoving his way down the street. I slumped against the potter's shop—a Roman whipping. I remembered a Roman soldier threatening several of us last summer after we accidentally hit a rock into the barracks courtyard when playing a game. He brought out a whip made of multiple leather thongs. There were metal barbs and balls tied to the ends of the thongs. He said not everyone survived a Roman whipping.

My body shook. I forced myself to breathe. Until that moment I hadn't realized I'd been holding my breath. Maybe father would let me watch the sheep with Uncle Roi until Magnus forgot about all this.

ᔒ ◆ ᔓ

I hurried home, intent on convincing father that I should spend more time in the field learning how to care for the sheep. As I approached our house I saw Uncle Roi carrying an injured lamb to the stable behind our house. Perfect. I would talk him into letting me help out in the fields and together he and I would convince father.

"Uzziel," he called. "Come."

I joined him in the stable as he tended to the lamb.

"I heard a Roman soldier was waiting for you after class."

"Shai, you unfaithful—"

My uncle held up his hand. "Now, now. Your cousin was just concerned."

"I suppose everyone knows."

"No. Just me."

I flopped down in the straw and stroked the animal's wool. "He saw me last night."

"After you saw the baby?"

I stared at him. "How'd you know?"

Uncle Roi laughed. "You forget I am a shepherd. I hear thieves and animals preying on my sheep."

"How did you know it was me following you?"

"I also see in the dark."

"So you knew I was following you?"

"Why do you think I led the other shepherds past our house? I knew you and Shai were sleeping on the roof."

"You wanted me to follow?"

"I hoped you both would."

The lamb bleated.

"So what did you think?" my uncle asked.

"He's a baby."

"Yes." He chuckled. "Every man except the first Adam starts off as an infant."

He sounded like Shai. "I know. I was just hoping for a strong military leader and king who will depose Herod the fake." I spat. "And run the Romans out of our land."

Uncle Roi nodded. "I understand. But we must be patient."

"I'm tired of being patient."

"Listen to you, oh man of many years. You are just a boy. Patience comes with age and wisdom. But we must be careful where Herod and the Romans are concerned."

"You sound like Rabbi Harel."

"He is a wise man, Uzziel. It wasn't that long ago, a year, maybe two since King Herod killed two of his own sons, Alexander and Aristobulus."

"He did?" I thought back to what I'd told Magnus.

"Yes, and he's killed others too. Herod is very jealous for the kingdom. It is safer to be a pig in Herod's household than a man. He fears anyone he thinks will take his kingdom from him."

My stomach churned.

"So what did you tell this Roman?"

I twisted a piece of straw.

"Uzziel?"

"That there was a lost child and people were looking for him."

"How long did it take you to weave that fable?"

"It just came out. Oh, did you see that bright star last night?"

"You're changing the conversation."

"But did you see it?"

"Yes. What do you think about it?"

"I think it's a sign. Remember the prophecy? 'I see him, but not now; I behold him, but not near. A star will come out of Jacob; a scepter will rise out of Israel. He will crush the foreheads of Moab, the skulls of all the people of Sheth, Edom will be conquered; Seir his enemy, will be conquered, but Israel will grow strong. A ruler will come out of Jacob and destroy the survivors of the city.' I never saw that star until last night."

"Neither have I."

"So do you think he's the promised Messiah?"

"Without a doubt, which is why we must be careful what we speak in public and especially to the Romans." He finished bandaging the lamb and stood. "Shall we go see him?"

"Who?"

"The Messiah. The women have prepared some food for us to take to Joseph and Mary."

"Afterward can I return to the fields with you?"

Uncle Roi shook his head. "No, I think your father needs you here for now."

A knot formed in my belly.

Chapter Four

Two Kingdoms

Uncle Roi, Shai, and I carried the food and a blanket to the little family. I kept an eye out for Magnus and whenever I saw a soldier my pace quickened. The streets were full of people here for the census so it was easier to avoid soldiers. Once again the man, Joseph, let us in.

Mary was grateful for the food and blanket. Shai and I sat near the baby. "Do you know who he is?" she asked.

"The Messiah," I said.

She smiled. "Your uncle told you?"

"Yes, but how do you know."

"An angel told us."

"An angel talked to you too?" Shai said.

"Yes."

The child stirred and awoke. She lifted him and placed the bundle in my arms.

He was so small. I couldn't believe I was actually holding our future king. It seemed impossible. Why me?

"What do you call him?" Shai asked.

"Joshua," the baby's mother whispered.

God is salvation, the meaning rang in my head. Last night the angels called him Messiah—the Anointed One—the Lord. I looked into his tiny face. "Will you save us from the Romans?"

His brown eyes stared back. An excitement simmered inside me.

Last night I didn't know who this baby was. Now I couldn't believe that Yahweh had blessed me to both see and hold the long awaited Savior. Knowing who this baby was made all the difference. Yahweh had placed this child in my arms for a reason. I would do all I could to see him come to power.

"I'll ask around," my uncle said.

I turned to see him and Joseph talking.

"I'm sure there's some place around here where you and your family can live."

"What about the home where the widow Tikva lived?" I said.

"No, Uzziel. I don't think that will work. Joseph here is a carpenter, he needs a shop."

"So maybe he could fix my loom?"

"I'd be glad to," Joseph said.

"It may take a few days or weeks," my uncle said to the child's father. "I think every available space is being used to house travelers for the census."

Joseph nodded. "I appreciate your help."

"Come Uzziel, Shai, it's time to go."

I handed my future king back to his mother. The mere thought that I held my king sent tingles up my spine.

We headed home. Several soldiers crossed before us when we reached the inn. I waited for them to pass. "Uncle Roi, what if the Romans find the baby?"

"We must be careful what we say, Uzziel. But I don't think they will. There are so many people coming and going right now that it would be almost impossible for them to differentiate him from all the other children roaming about."

I smiled with relief.

"He is the Messiah and I'm sure Yahweh will protect him. But we should also pray to that end."

℘ ◆ ℭ

I waited in the ravine for Shai and the others to arrive. One of the boys stood on the hill across from me. He was my sentry and gave a raven's call whenever someone outside our group approached. The boys were to enter a few at a time. No more than three together and from different directions.

We'd been meeting here for nearly a month. Though some argued that it would be years before our Messiah would need us to usher him into power I countered that the more prepared we were the less work we would have later. Besides, I figured we'd need many more men and therefore I was training them as leaders to go into other towns to recruit and train warriors.

Most of them liked the idea of being commanders, though there were those like Shai who I'd determined were never destined for leadership. But I would deal with that when the time came. We spent several weeks crafting our weapons which we hid in a cave. Now we practiced shooting bow and arrows, throwing spears, and striking objects with our slingshots. We had all improved, especially with our slingshots.

The boys arrived and stood in two straight lines as I paced before them like I'd seen the Roman commanders do by the barracks.

"Men, as you know, this land belongs to us Jews. The Romans try to impress their rule over us but we will not be wax for Caesar's signet ring. They think because they have the power they can take the best food, the best cloth, the best homes, tax us, and leave us to starve. Well, not for long. We will rebel. We will work to make—"

"Uzziel," Shai's eyes were wide and his face pale.

"Shai, how many times have I told you to call me captain?"

"But Uzziel," another boy said.

It was then I noticed the frightened look on all their faces. Pebbles crushed behind me. I turned to see Magnus with my scout trembling in front of the soldier's javelin.

"Don't stop on account of me, Captain Uzziel," the soldier said, sunlight reflecting off his helmet and body armor.

"Oh, well, we're just pretending." I glared at my scout. How could he allow the enemy to just sneak up on us like this?

"Pretending that you're going to defeat the Roman army?" A deep thunderous laugh burst from Magnus. "For over a thousand years the Romans have ruled the world. I serve under the command that my father, my grandfather, and my great grandfather have served under. If you think you little Jewish boys can defeat the mighty Roman army you are sadly mistaken."

We stood silent. Each examining the dirt beneath our feet.

"But I must say, I am impressed with your efforts. Maybe I can convince you to join our mighty legion and serve the Emperor. That way at least you'll be on the winning side."

I brooded. Never would I join the Romans.

Magnus looked me in the eye. "So you want to play soldiers and fight us Romans," he said. "Then I think it only fair for you to see what you are up against."

He marched us to the soldiers' barracks and gave us a tour, flaunting the weapons with which they oppressed us into submission. We looked in awe at the large number of swords and javelins neatly hanging from hooks. He showed us the gladius sword, longer than most of our arms. "Uzziel, see if you can swing this spathia." He handed me an even longer sword and though I swung it, I knew its weight would grow weary in my slender arms.

There were full body shields, a large stockpile of heavy pilum javelins each with long thin iron shanks and a heavy shaft.

"This is a hasta," Magnus said lifting a spear that, when the wood shaft was set on the ground, rose above his head. "We can thrust this through a shield and impale the enemy on the other side of that shield."

Our eyes widened at this news.

"Even if the soldier at the end of the point—" Magnus lowered the spear to touch its iron sharp edge. "—isn't killed, his shield is destroyed." Magnus smiled. "Then, it's only a matter of time."

The boys I'd assembled as future military leaders drew back.

"For close, hand-to-hand combat we use the pugio." He unsheathed a dagger about the length of my forearm. It had a wide blade shaped like a leaf.

There was a collective "ah" from the boys.

Magnus continued his tour. "We also have light-weight throwing javelins and bows."

We all admired the sturdy bows made of wood and horn. I could only imagine the accuracy and thrill of shooting such a weapon.

All about us soldiers milled about, cleaning and sharpening their weapons and laughing heartily when Magnus told them what we were planning.

Then, he led us into the jail, a cave really. It was small. I assumed they didn't expect large numbers of criminals in our small town. They had assessed correctly. The jail was cold and dark; the air stale and foul. Men coughed and torches gave off sooty light. When the prisoners saw us they scrambled to the gates of their cells. Their hands—limited by chains—grasped at us.

We shrank from their touch and formed a tight cluster in the narrow passageway.

Magnus laughed. It was obvious he delighted in the tour. "This worthless criminal stole a sheep."

A haggard man with long fingernails gripped the bars of his cage.

I cringed at the sight of him and wondered if he'd stolen the sheep from my family's flock or Yahweh's.

"This snake refused to pay his taxes."

"You Romans have taxed us so hard we can't even feed our families." The man shook with his anger. "Yahweh will judge you."

"Shut up old man."

We passed two other men, their deeds exposed to us.

I hoped we were done. I really had no desire to go on. The last thing I wanted was to see *him*. But Magnus continued his tour. He seemed to get more and more pleasure from every prisoner he introduced us to. When we reached the darkest part of the jail he stopped.

There stood an old man, his gray beard matted and crawling with lice. I recognized him at once and glanced away. I wanted to ask Magnus if we could go, but I was sure that would only mean a longer stay.

"This is our most important prisoner," Magnus said with a grin.

"Help me, lads. Help me. Please. I'm innocent," the man called, his voice raspy.

Magnus drew his dagger and brought it to the iron gate.

The man dropped back.

"Grovel you filthy dog."

The prisoner trembled.

I cringed and dared not make eye contact. I was certain if I did he would know it was me.

"If it were up to me," Magnus said, his blade inserted into the man's cell. "You'd be crucified by now."

I felt the cool walls press in on me.

"I was just traveling through the hills that day. I didn't hit that soldier."

"But you had a slingshot," Magnus shot back.

"Of course I did. There are bears, lions, and robbers on that trail. A man must protect himself."

My stomach churned and my head spun. Bile rose to my mouth and I forced it back down.

My cousin and friends exchanged looks. According to what I'd been telling them, this man was a hero. If only he was guilty.

"Obviously somebody believes your story old man." Magnus turned to us. "Don't waste your time trying to fight us. You'll end up here." He paused and looked us each in the eyes. "Or dead."

"Can we go, sir?" one of my friends asked.

"Yes. But if I catch you planning to attack us, you'll stay longer. Much longer." He led us out of the jail.

"Yes, sir," my friends said and several others nodded.

I breathed a sigh of relief once in the sunshine. I turned to go but Magnus put his hand on my shoulder and squeezed. "Not so soon, Uzziel. I've been listening to your people. Seems you weren't completely honest with me."

The chill from the jail wrapped itself around me like a chain. "What do you mean, sir?"

"The child hadn't wandered off, it was a newborn."

"Oh."

"And not just any newborn."

"Really?"

"Really. And I think you know that."

"Well, you know how gossip goes."

"Who was that child, Uzziel?" His thumb and fingers pressed into the muscles of my shoulder as if trying to touch each other.

"Our future king," I spat. "The one who's going to kick you Romans out of our land."

Magnus laughed. The sound filled the barracks courtyard. Other soldiers stopped to watch with smug looks of superiority. "You people are so delusional. Don't you know Caesar is God?"

I wrestled free of his filthy grip and ran. Our king would free us from their oppression. Magnus and his fellow soldiers would see. And I would do all I could to see that happen.

OF GREAT MEN

AND JEALOUSY

Chapter Five

Stop Them

"Catch me."

I looked up to see the carpenter's son leap from a low branch on the olive tree outside their door. "Ugh." I wrapped my arms around the toddler. "Joshua ben Joseph." My heart pounded against my chest. "You scared me."

He grinned and wiggled down.

"How did you get up there?"

"I climb. Look. Look." He pulled me over to a small mound of stones below the tree. "Look, I form."

"Yes, nice pile."

He looked intently into my eyes. "No." Joshua picked up a stone from the pile. "I form." He turned to the tree. "I form." He pointed. He pulled an insect off the tree and held it up. "I form."

I chuckled. "Joshua you are—"

He looked past me, down the street, his face serious. "No." He pointed.

Behind me the sound of feet, voices, shouts, and weeping. I turned to see a crowd approaching, several Roman soldiers in their midst.

"No," Joshua said, his voice more emphatic.

A panic seized me as the crowd came into view. I scooped Joshua up and held him close.

"They're going to kill him, they're going to kill him," several boys shouted as they ran past.

There, in the middle of the crowd, beaten, bloody, and carrying a large rough piece of wood was the old man from the prison. His gray beard matted with patches of red skin where the soldiers had pulled handfuls out.

Joshua ben Joseph's small hands pressed my cheeks. "No," he repeated, his brown eyes staring deep into mine. "No kill. Stop them, Uzziel, stop them."

A shiver spread across my back and down my arms. Did he understand what was happening? How could he?

Mary, the boy's mother, came out and took Joshua into her arms.

"Uzziel," Chaim, my friend called. "They're crucifying the old man." He grabbed my arm and pulled me along.

I glanced back at Joshua, his face contorted into grief and pain—a look that mirrored my heart. My legs stumbled under me, unwilling to move they grew heavier with every step.

How could this be happening?

"I'm innocent," the old man squawked, his voice hoarse and desperate. His claim the same as two years ago when we'd seen him in the prison. His story hadn't changed. Why should it? He told the truth—I should know.

People jostled against me, every touch a slap of rebuke, a nudge to make this right. *"No kill. Stop them, Uzziel, stop them."* The small boy's words repeated in my mind, growing larger like rings on a lake after a stone is thrown, never to be retrieved.

My friend Chaim dragged me along with the crowd. Their words, the scuff of their sandals on the hard ground scraped against my nerves. The smell of the crowd, their hot breath on my skin, their weeping, all of it turned my stomach. Would they weep if it was me carrying the crossbar?

This man had done nothing to deserve this. He was their scapegoat.

The man turned and looked at me.

No. He was my scapegoat. A chill ran through my flesh. "Why are they killing him now?" I asked my friend.

"Magnus has convinced the captain that the old man is guilty."

"How?"

"I don't know." Chaim looked at me. "Are you well?"

"No. They shouldn't be killing him. He's innocent."

"Uzziel, you're the one who always said he was a hero."

"He is, he's a hero for suffering under Roman oppression. But he's innocent."

We stopped and the crowd moved around us like water around a snag.

"How do you know?"

My teeth chattered in spite of the warm air. "I...I...I just do."

Chaim swiped his hand through the air. "You've just been listening to his rantings." He turned and followed the crowd.

"No. No I'm not. He's innocent."

Several people looked at me as they passed.

"No kill. Stop them, Uzziel, stop them." How could I? *"...stop them."* Goose flesh rose on my skin. *"...stop them."* I ran to catch up with the crowd. "Excuse me, excuse me." I worked my way through.

"Excuse me."

A burly man shouldered back. "Stop your shoving. A man is about to lose his life and all you can think of is getting to the front to watch?"

My breath caught in my chest. How could he possibly think such a thing? I stepped back, and was bumped into from behind. I moved further to the man's right and again worked my way through the crowd.

We exited the village and proceeded down the hill on the main Roman highway north, to Jerusalem. It was easier now to pass people and make my way forward. Closer to the old man and the solders. Closer to my own fate. I tried to push that out of my mind.

I glimpsed the old man, his tunic filthy, torn, and bloody. My pace slowed.

Someone pushed me from behind.

"Stop them, Uzziel, stop them."

I took a deep breath and pressed forward. I was now only ten paces behind him.

A soldier poked the criminal in the ribs with his javelin. "Hurry up old man. I'd like to get home in time for supper."

"Stop." The word escaped my lips before I knew I'd said it.

The soldier turned. Magnus.

All around me others slowed and sound drifted away like sheared wool falling from a lamb.

"What'd you say?"

Around me the crowd's stares weighed against me. "I…I…I said—"

"Speak, Uzziel."

"Stop." My voice was weak and wavering. "Stop. Don't hurt him."

Magnus laughed. "What's a little pain before death?"

"Don't."

"Don't what? Don't do this?" The soldier rammed his javelin into the old man's side again.

The man doubled. Blood ran.

"No. Don't. He's innocent."

Magnus glared at me. In four swift strides he loomed over me. "What makes you say that?"

I stared into his hardened face. "He, he just is."

His face contorted and he squinted at me. "Is there something you're not telling me, Uuuzzieeel?"

Here it was. My opportunity to lift the heavy burden I'd carried for three years. *"Stop them, Uzziel, stop them."* But to lift a heavy burden also meant death—a horrible death.

Chaim sidled up beside me. "Uzziel, what are you doing?" He grabbed my arms and tried to pull me away.

"No." I struggled to free myself. "He's innocent. I—"

"Speak."

"I—I threw—"

"Uzziel." My father pushed through the crowd to reach me. "What are you doing?"

"This man is innocent. I should be—"

"You should be at home."

Magnus grinned. "Listen to your father, Captain Uzziel. Only a foolish boy steps in the way of a Roman execution."

My father glared at me. "Uzziel, go home."

"Father, I—"

"I said, 'go home.' "

I looked at the old man, his gaze intent on me. A shade of hope lay lightly across his face. How many nights had I awakened with his desperate expression carved into my dreams? Now, right now I could put an end to those haunting visions.

Magnus jabbed his javelin into my side. "You want to join the old man?"

Warm blood spread across my inner tunic. "No, I. I mean, don't kill him."

"Go home, boy."

"Come, Uzziel." My father's hands gripped my shoulders and turned my body.

I searched for the old man in the crowd. His face now downcast as hope slid to the dirt.

"Move, old man," Magnus shouted.

People whispered as we passed.

As we approached Migdal Eder I heard the first strike of the hammer against the nail followed by the man's scream. My stomach reeled and I wretched.

Chapter Six

Trouble In Disguise

I awoke drenched in sweat, my body shaking. Another nightmare. Every night since the old man's crucifixion vivid and haunting dreams plagued my sleep. Sometimes I took the cross from him, offering him the hope of deliverance, only to thrust the cross back at him. Other times I hung on the cross and he looked up at me.

But tonight I dreamed of the Day of Atonement. I dreamed of the goat slain for our sins and the scapegoat taken into the wilderness to remove our guilt.

Could my sin ever be covered? How many goats must die to cleanse me from this man's blood? How many goats must wander, alone, in the wilderness to remove my guilt?

I climbed the stairs to the roof. For some reason this place gave me a small sense of peace. I looked out over Bethlehem. The fields beyond were dotted white in the moonlight with flocks of sacrificial lambs. Sometimes I wanted to walk out into the fields and wander away, never to return. I guess I always knew the old man might die, but I had always told myself it wouldn't happen.

I turned my gaze from the fields to the sky. The bright star that appeared two years ago seemed brighter and closer. Just last night it hovered to the north, probably somewhere near Jerusalem. Now it seemed even closer, as though it were moving right toward me.

I sat on the low wall that fenced our roof and watched it. The star shimmered and danced. It was so much bigger than it had been two years ago when Joshua ben Joseph was born. Even bigger—no closer than several months ago.

Recollections of that night surfaced. Shai and I attempting to sleep on the roof. Below, travelers here for the Roman census slept on our mats inside. My uncle and the other shepherds wandering through our village in the middle of the night. Myself following them to the tower of the flock where little Joshua, all bundled up in cloths, lay in one of the mangers where the shepherds usually laid the temple lambs.

How I'd grown to love that babe, now a small boy. There was something special about him. In some ways I felt as though I had a special connection to him. I'd seen him the night he'd been born. The night the angels told my uncle Roi and the other shepherds about him.

Because of the message to the shepherds, many in Bethlehem took special pride in him. Why shouldn't we? Didn't the prophet say, "But you, Bethlehem Ephrathah, though you are small among the clans of Judah, out of you will come for me one who will be ruler over Israel, whose origins are from of old, from days of eternity"?

Yes, we were proud of him and secretly hoped we would be part of his new kingdom when he rose to power and shook the Romans from the folds of Israel.

Because I believed he was the promised Messiah I made sure to visit him as often as I could, usually two or three times a week. I did, that is, until the old man died. Now, I just couldn't bring myself to see him. Joshua had implored me to stop the old man's crucifixion. As odd as it seemed, even though Joshua was a child, I felt as though he knew the man was innocent.

A few days ago, I had actually tried to go see him. But as I walked toward the carpenter's home I heard the pounding of a hammer on nail. I stopped, frozen to the ground, and pressed my fingernails into my wrists. A sharp cry pierced my ears. I looked up to see little Joshua peering out the window at me. He reached his little hands out to me, but I ran away. I wanted to see him, but I had failed him. In spite of his pleas the old man was dead. I was too weak to acknowledge my guilt.

Now, up on our roof, I stared out to Migdal Eder, the tower of the flock. That's when I saw them. A large caravan moving toward Bethlehem on the road from Jerusalem. Who was it? Were they

Romans? Was there some sort of trouble? Were Herod and his wives traveling to the Herodium, the palace he'd built to the southeast of Bethlehem?

As I watched them approach, I realized that, though there appeared to be soldiers of some sort, they weren't Roman. The group moved in an even, organized way, eliminating the idea that they might be thieves or a band of rebels fighting the Romans.

I realized the star was not behind this group but in front of them. In fact, it was between me and the approaching group. The star hung so low in the sky it hovered over the—no it almost touched the carpenter's home.

I stretched to see. Yes, it was the home of Joshua, our little Messiah.

I watched as the caravan passed through the gate. A dog barked, and then another. Occasionally I caught a glimpse of the travelers riding upon camels followed by a long line of other camels carrying all the necessities for travel with servants and guards walking alongside.

Just like that night two years earlier I slipped down the stairs into the street and made my way to the carpenter's house. Others heard the commotion of all these strangers traversing our streets and peered through latticed windows or slightly opened doors. A few ventured out and stood in the shadows.

In front of the carpenter's house, a group of men, dressed different than any I'd ever seen, dismounted. As they did, servants gathered about them, brushing desert sand and dust off the men's richly ornamented robes. Other servants filled bowls with water and proceeded to wash and groom the travelers. All the while, these distinguished men spoke together in solemn tones.

A servant near me unloaded items from a camel.

I looked for one of the men standing guard with a drawn sword, but the nearest guard seemed preoccupied. I slowly approached a servant. "Sir," I bowed to the man.

He stopped and stared at me.

"My name is Uzziel. How may I be of service to you and your masters?"

"Javed." A guard stood beside the man, his gaze intent on me. "Does this commoner bother you?"

The servant looked at me. "What do you want boy?"

I gulped; the man with the sword looked fit and strong. "Who are you sirs? And why have you come?"

"We are from the region of Parthia and have traveled long distances for many months to see and worship the King of the Jews."

I stared at him, unable to speak. Parthia, a land far to the east. I'd heard of these people from father who met all kinds of people in his travels to Jerusalem. They were a strong and wise people, independent of the Romans.

Joseph, the carpenter must have heard the ruckus and stepped outside to investigate.

At Joseph's appearance, every member of the entourage bowed before him.

Joseph, a quiet, humble man, was unnerved by the visitors' response.

One of the men arose. "Sir, I and my companions have traveled a long distance to worship the King of the Jews."

Joseph's eyes widened and he surveyed the group and growing crowd of neighbors. "Come, he is in here." Joseph opened the door and light spilled into the street. The man entered and was followed by others.

"What's going on?" someone whispered behind me.

I turned to Javed. "Can I help you?"

The guard looked me over.

"Untie that rope." He pointed to a camel loaded with bundles.

I hurried to the creature, and did as I was told. I'd never seen a camel up close. "How did you know our Messiah was born?"

"The men inside worshiping your king are wise men, scholars. They study many ancient texts including a prophecy of Balaam about a star and writings from your prophet Daniel who lived in our country. In those writings they were told that when a great star appeared it would signal the birth of a mighty king. So when they saw the star—" He pointed to the star now directly over the small house. "They searched their scrolls and charts and determined this star was that sign spoken of so long ago."

A shiver of nervous excitement crept over me. How great would this small child become that Yahweh foretold his birth to these Gentiles from so far away?

"When he was born angels told our shepherds of his birth," I told Javed as I helped him.

"You must tell that to the Magi." He grabbed a small chest and motioned for me to take the other side. "Be careful, this is heavy."

I helped him unload the ornate box from the camel. "What are all these containers?"

"Gifts for the king. Surely you have given him gifts."

Heat flushed up my neck, cheeks, and ears. I was thankful for the darkness, which covered my shame.

❧ ♦ ☙

The Magi set up a camp outside town. Over the next several days various men would come to the carpenter's house and talk with Joseph and Mary about the child, bringing gifts of gold, frankincense, and myrrh, among other things.

I thought about what Javed said. I had been so excited about how the Messiah would free us from the Romans that I hadn't thought about bringing him a gift. I tried to think about what I could give him. I didn't have anything as nice as what the Magi brought him.

Shai and I delivered food that our mothers sent to Mary to feed her guests. While there, I noticed Joshua holding a gold coin one of the men had given him. "I form," he said and ran over to me and Shai to show us.

On our way home, Magnus stepped from the shadows where he'd watched two more of the Magi enter the small home. "What are those travelers doing here?"

I startled, engrossed in the excitement.

Several people that were loitering about scurried off when they saw the Roman soldier.

"They're here to worship our king," I said, surprised by the boldness in my voice.

Shai nudged me, as if to say: *Shush, don't tell him.*

"Huh. There's no king here. You people are delusional. The closest king is Herod. If they want to worship a king they should worship Herod or Caesar."

I seethed inside. Someday soon, our Messiah would rule over us and these Romans would no longer ruin our lives.

CHAPTER SEVEN

STOLEN HOPE

Loud voices, screams, cries, and the pounding of horses' hooves awoke me early one morning, several days after the Magi had left.

I arose. With father gone, I was now in charge. Father left two days earlier with a wagon full of cloth. He followed the same path south which the Magi traveled. I thought it odd that the Magi left from a different direction in which they'd come, away from Jerusalem.

With the Magi gone, life had settled back to normal. But what was this?

Already, several of my younger siblings had joined the cacophony of crying.

"What is happening?" Orel, my seven year-old brother, asked.

"I'm scared," Maayan said and reached for me.

I lifted his small body into my arms. He was older than the Messiah by only a few months. I wondered if they would play together in a few years.

"Uzziel," My mother appeared in the doorway of the small room I shared with my brothers. "Go find out what is happening and come back. *Quickly!*"

I handed Maayan to my sister, Kelila, and ran out the door. In the street there was chaos. A woman holding a small child fled toward me with a Roman soldier gaining on her. The woman bumped into me and fell down.

I reached down to help her up. "What's happening?"

The look on her face screamed fear. Once on her feet, she took several steps, but the fall had cost her valuable time.

The soldier grabbed her by the hair and yanked her back. "You lousy, filthy Jew. You thought you could run from a Roman soldier?" He spat in her face and seized the crying child from her arms.

"No, please no." She grabbed for the boy.

The soldier shoved her back, then plunged a knife into the child's belly, sliced his chest open, and threw him to the ground.

The woman crumpled to her feet. She scooped up the child and wept over him.

I stared in horror.

The soldier turned to a door that had just slammed shut and kicked it open.

I caught a glimpse of a father slipping into an alley, a small child in his arms.

A soldier on a horse galloped toward us. I grabbed the weeping mother at my feet. "Come." She wouldn't budge.

The horse sped closer.

"My baby, my son."

I pulled at her again.

"Go away." She swatted at me.

I jumped out of the horse's way as it sped past—its rider kicked at the mother's head.

A man ran after the soldier and hurled a rock at him.

"What are they doing?"

The man stared at me. "They're killing all our sons, two years and under."

Maayan, Adi, Chesed—I must protect them. I ran up the street to our home. As I passed a neighbor's house a soldier exited, blood covered his clothes, hands, legs, and dagger. Inside the house I heard screaming and sobbing. All around me, mayhem. I burst through our door. My mother and sister sat huddled in a corner with all the children. The house was dark as mother had closed all the shutters.

"What is it Uzziel? What is happening?"

"They're killing the boys."

She stared at me, my words not making sense.

"Come, we must hide them." I grabbed Maayan and led my family to the inner courtyard. Bashe, my Uncle Roi's wife, and her two daughters huddled under a palm tree in the corner. My cousin Shai entered from his family's living quarters opposite ours.

"Get Chesed," I told him. "We must hide him. The wool." I pointed to a huge pile we stored in another corner, all washed and ready to be spun into thread and woven into the cloth that father sold.

I lifted the bundle. "Orel, Maayan, get back there. Mother, go, hide with Adi."

She shook her head. "No, you hide." She thrust Adi into Kelila's arms and ordered us both to hide behind the wool.

In the streets soldiers shouted. Children cried. Mothers screamed.

Bashe stood and pulled her girls to the wool.

I looked at little Noy, not yet two years old, her hair in short curls about her head. Shai arrived with his sister and two brothers and they huddled in the corner.

"Mother." Shai's youngest brother stood to go to his mother.

"Chesed, no. You must stay," Shai ordered

Several children resumed their crying.

The sounds of metal striking bone and cobblestone seeped into the courtyard.

Shai and I had just grabbed the wool to pull it over us when a soldier banged on the front door. Seconds later the door splintered open and the sounds from the street poured in.

I held Maayan tight, my hand over his mouth as his body writhed in mine. Shai did the same with Chesed.

"Shush," Kelila whispered.

"Be still," I ordered.

Water pots and bowls crashed in the house as the soldier turned over mother's work table. "Get out here," he ordered.

Outside our hiding place Bashe and Shai's mother pushed the wool over us.

I heard my mother say something to the soldier.

"Where are they woman?"

There was a loud slap, thump, and cry. I tensed, knowing the soldier had hit my mother, the force of the impact knocking her body into a wall. I held Maayan tighter to keep myself from springing from our hiding place and attacking the brute.

"Where are your children?"

I could tell he was now in our courtyard. My aunts whimpered. A door banged open. Maayan bit my hand. Instinctively I pulled it away and he cried. I clamped my hand back over his mouth. He bit down again and I squeezed back tears.

Within moments my mother and aunts screamed and the morning light, filtered out by the wool, seeped in as the soldier flung our covering away from us.

"No, No." Bashe fell at the man's feet. "Why? Why do you kill our babies?"

The soldier kicked her aside. "Herod's orders. All boys two and younger."

"But why?"

The soldier came at us. I, Kelila, and Shai clung to the younger children who now screamed in terror. He yanked little Adi from Kelila's arms, his large hand wrapped tightly around my baby brother's neck. There was a crush of bone and the soldier dropped Adi, now silent, into my sister's lap. Kelila screamed, her hands poised above our dead brother, afraid to touch him.

Little Noy wailed and the soldier grabbed her. She screamed louder, and struggled in his arms.

Bashe leapt at the soldier. "She's a girl. She's a girl."

The soldier glared at Bashe then ripped Noy's tunic.

I shuddered at the disgrace of this gentile male exposing my niece—a shame she will wear the rest of her life.

He flung Noy down and Bashe caught her before she struck the stones.

The soldier yanked Chesed from Shai's hands.

Shai scrambled to his feet and made a grab for his brother.

With one quick movement, the soldier severed Chesed's small head and flung the child's limp body at Shai.

Shai's mother crumpled to the ground. Shai instinctively grabbed his brother and now looked in horror at the bloody body in his arms. All around me wailing and cries of fear sucked the oxygen from the air.

The smell of blood filled my nostrils. My stomach spasmed. Mayaan struggled free and ran to mother. He never made it.

⅋ ♦ ⅌

I climbed the stairs to the roof of our home. The image of my mother staring blankly into our hushed home filled my mind. I avoided looking at her. The wet spots on the outside of her tunic, reminders that Adi was no longer around to nurse and my guilt that I had failed to protect Adi, Maayan, and even Chesed weighed on me like wet wool.

I had cried so much in the past two weeks my eyes felt dry and empty of tears.

On the roof, I stared out over our sad village. The bright colored clothing people had once worn to express their joy and love of life was now absent. Instead, we wore sackcloth or garments torn to represent our grief. Shiva, the week of mourning after burial, had ended and we were now in the Shloshim, the period of re-entry into the world of the living. But the grief, both individually and as a community, kept us in the world of the dead.

All of our baby boys were dead. Several parents and grandparents who had fought to protect their children were also among those in the grave. Why the Romans had swooped upon us like wolves upon a flock of helpless sheep we couldn't discern.

As the sun set, smoke from cook fires spiraled into the clear night. Where usually there was laughter and conversation, the evening was quiet; until the sound of a wail arose answered by the cry of another. Soon all about me an offering of lament lifted to Yahweh—some sharp and clear, others muffled and discreet. The goats we kept for milk bleated and somewhere a donkey brayed. It seemed all of Bethlehem mourned.

I looked out to the fields where I knew my uncle Roi and the other shepherds grazed the sheep. How I wished I could be with them—away from all this grief and guilt, though I knew it would follow me like a lost lamb.

"You are not to blame," my father had told me.

But still, I felt as though I should have done more—fought that soldier at least. Though it seemed I was not as brave when face-to-face with a Roman soldier as I believed myself to be.

A noise behind me interrupted my thoughts. I turned to see Orel. He was thinner than just two weeks ago. Weren't we all? Kelila and I had taken to preparing food as Mother was unable to rouse herself to the task.

"Show me the star," Orel asked and slipped his arm around my waist.

"Of course." I turned to the spot where it hovered above the carpenter's home and extended my hand. I stopped.

"What is it?"

I stared in unbelief. "No. Yahweh. No."

Orel gazed in the direction I had pointed. "Where is it?"

My skin turned cold. "It is. . ." I scanned the sky to see if it had moved. "It's gone."

I grabbed Orel's hand and we ran down the stairs and into the street.

"Where are we going?"

"To the carpenter's house."

"Uzziel. Slow down."

I tried to slow my pace. We reached the house and it was dark. I pushed the door open. From the light of the moon I could make out a work table and several upturned pots and baskets. "Joseph, Mary. Where are you?"

"They are gone."

I turned to see a neighbor man standing in the doorway.

"Where are they?"

"I don't know. All I know is they are gone."

"When did they leave?"

"I do not know."

I slumped against a wall. "Joshua ben Joseph—is he dead?"

"I suppose," said the neighbor. "The soldiers came on Herod's orders to kill the one born King of the Jews."

I froze at this revelation. "No. No, they couldn't kill Joshua. He is our Messiah."

The man shrugged. "All I know is they killed all the male children two and under and he was two."

Questions swirled in my mind but no words passed my lips.

"Messiah or not," continued the man. "The carpenter and his wife are gone." He turned and walked away.

Tears swelled, a reserve I didn't know existed.

Orel sat down next to me. "The Messiah—is he dead?"

I sniffled and wrapped my arm around him. Together we cried.

We thought ourselves blessed to have the Messiah born and living here in our village. We were unaware of the price we would pay for such a blessing.

CONFLICTING

PATHS

CHAPTER EIGHT

TWO PATHS

Jerusalem, 30 A.D.

"**D**o you think we'll see him, Father?" my son asked.

"See who?" I stepped from the booth my family slept in for the Feast of Tabernacles.

"You know?"

"My cousin, Shai?" I teased and cinched tight a small money pouch.

"No." Natan feigned exasperation. "The Teacher. Remember Hillel's story of the Teacher healing the lame man at the Pool of Bethesda?"

I nodded, remembering this and many other stories that people in our tiny village of Bethlehem had heard over the past few years. They were stories people talked of often.

"Do you think we'll see him? Surely, he's here at the feast."

I shrugged. "It's possible." I thought of the rumors that thousands of people followed this teacher into the wilderness where he healed the sick and taught. People who'd heard him said he really cared for the people. Something that could not be said of the Romans.

"Our host says this teacher comes and goes like the wind," I cautioned against disappointment. "He may be here for a day or a week. No one knows."

Odd that he should move about so much. Yet there was apparently a charisma that drew people to this man. I saw that he inspired hope in the hearts of many people. And behind closed doors, people believed he would overthrow the Romans.

"Can I go with the other boys to look for him?" Natan's face glowed with excitement.

Ah, to be young and idealistic. And why not? There was an excitement in the air. All around people spoke of this teacher, though not everyone agreed. Some said he was a good man while others said he deceived the people. Oddly, he had the religious leaders wringing their hands and threatening to arrest if not kill him.

All this excitement reminded me of a time in my own childhood, some thirty years ago, when I and all of Bethlehem felt a similar excitement. It had been years since I'd thought of that night, sleeping on the rooftop with my cousin, Shai. That night I'd slipped down to the street and followed my Uncle Roi and his shepherds to discover the one we thought was the promised Messiah.

I sighed at the thought of that happy night.

So much had happened since then—the morning Roman soldiers appeared, swords swinging. There was nowhere to run. Nowhere to hide. Like wolves they took the weakest and most vulnerable. Before the sun was high in the sky, all the boys two-years old and younger were dead. Many a parent and grandparent too.

After that day, my mother was never the same. So many people in our village were dead—their bodies just didn't know to stop living.

"Father?" Natan awoke me from my thoughts. "Can I go?"

"Yes." I smiled. "But then I want you to meet me in the temple courts, before the sun is high."

"Yes, Father."

I watched him run off. He was my youngest and growing up so quickly. Would he spend his whole life under Roman oppression as I had? Not if I had anything to say about it. I stuffed the coin pouch under my girdle and made ready to leave my host's courtyard.

"Uzziel," my host called as I neared the door. "I want to get your opinion on something."

I turned to my host. "Speak friend."

"Even in Bethlehem, you have heard of this teacher, no?"

"The miracle worker?"

He nodded. "You know, Uzziel, I once had the opportunity to hear the Teacher speak. His teaching, it is different than the teachers of the Law. This teacher, he speaks with such certainty and authority. When you hear him speak, it is as though his words are wind that blows away the cumbersome traditions of our elders that we may see clearly the heart of a matter, while at the same time, encasing the truth within an oyster shell that one must work hard to pry open."

"From your speech it sounds as though you are taking lessons from him."

My host chuckled and motioned for me to sit in the shade of his booth. "I'll give you an example. It is something I heard him say and have mulled over for quite some time."

I settled on a cushion and his wife brought us some goat's milk.

"The time I heard him he sat on a hillside and taught to a large crowd. He spoke about many things, murder, adultery, divorce, prayer, caring for the needy, and loving your enemies."

At the latter I raised an eyebrow. "Love your enemies?"

"Yes, and it is along these lines that I wish to consult you. I've heard you debate with the Sadducees. I know Yahweh has given you a good mind."

I waved him off. "I am a mere businessman, my friend."

"I've often wondered why no Rabbi ever took you in as his disciple."

"My family was crushed when the Romans killed my two brothers. How could I seek such an honor and leave them?"

My host nodded, his long white beard wagging as he did. "This teacher," he continued. "He said those who mourn are blessed for they will be comforted. That the meek are blessed, for they will inherit the earth."

I swirled the milk in my cup then took a long draw. I was unsure how to respond to such odd sayings.

"Think about these words Uzziel. I'd like to hear your thoughts."

I rubbed my chin. "I will contemplate them," I said.

"Good." He grabbed my hand and squeezed it. "I look forward to our discussion."

I left for the temple, my hand pressed to the coin pouch under my tunic. But first, I had a man to meet.

As I navigated the bustling streets of Jerusalem, I pondered the words of my host. "Blessed are the meek?" I muttered. Since when did the meek inherit anything? Let alone the earth? The meek mourned while the aggressors trampled and killed. How could anyone love such enemies? As for me, I would do what I could to see these detestable Roman scoured from our streets and land.

I checked to see I wasn't followed before I turned into a narrow alley. Three knocks on a low door brought a brusque voice, "Who requests entry?"

"A friend of the people."

"Whose people?"

"The true people," I replied.

An old woman opened the door ever so slightly. She looked me up and down then let me in.

She escorted me through a dimly lit room to a courtyard crowded with booths made of branches. The old woman led me to the largest of the booths, where a group of men lounged on pillows. Bowls and clay pots sat on the ground where a table would normally be.

A sinewing man with a cut under his right eye stood. "Ah, Uzziel. It is good to see you." He embraced me and kissed both cheeks. "Join us will you?"

I sat and took the bread Barabbas offered.

"How are you, my brother?" the man asked.

"I am well. And you?"

"Chased day and night by those Roman dogs. Their ever watchful eyes hinder me and my men from celebrating the feast."

I nodded, having heard the rumors of his exploits and clashes, as well as the threats of the Romans who wanted him and his band of rebels jailed and crucified.

"Tell me, Barabbas, what do you think of this teacher everyone is following?"

A dark cloud appeared to cover Barabbas' face. "I don't trust him."

"Why? The people seem to adore him."

"The people are fools. They care nothing for our traditions."

"Expound."

"I take it you have not heard him."

"I was hoping I might see him during the feast."

"He encourages—no outright breaks the Sabbath."

I stopped eating. "How so?"

"He heals people on the Sabbath. Aren't there six other days during the week he could heal? He also has no problem with his disciples failing to ceremonially wash their hands."

Now that I thought about it, Hillel did say the Teacher healed the lame man by the pool on the Sabbath. I considered this.

"From what I can tell, he's more interested in arguing with the religious leaders than confronting the Romans."

"You don't think he'll chase out the Romans?"

Barabbas shook his head.

I found this disheartening. "But we've got to get rid of these brute invaders." I slid the bag of coins to him.

He took it and smiled. "We'll get rid of them."

"We will." I stood. "We will chase those Roman dogs into the sea."

CHAPTER NINE

GLIMPSES

I entered the temple courts to find it more crowded than usual. A large group clustered around a man who sat teaching. I noticed many of the religious leaders dressed in their long flowing robes cloistered in small groups apart from the crowd. They appeared to be eying with contempt the simply clothed teacher.

"Why are all these people here so early?" I asked a man standing on the edge of the crowd.

"To hear the Teacher," he pointed at the speaker, a man ten or so years younger than I.

As the man next to me spoke I noticed a smile of eager expectation spread across his lips. "Have you heard him?"

"No."

"Oh, he is surely a prophet. He speaks like no other and it has been said that he has healed the lame and blind and even raised the dead."

"Raised the dead?" I couldn't believe such a thing, though I too had heard these rumors.

"Oh yes, on more than one occasion."

"Is this the man they call Jesus?"

"He is."

I worked my way into the crowd and had just sat down to listen when a commotion to my right drew all our attention. A group of teachers and Pharisees approached dragging a woman who struggled in their grip.

"No, no," she protested. "Please have mercy on me. I'm not alone in this. Please, no." She wept and leaned away from the men who roughly escorted her.

Some in the crowd craned their necks, others stood. I noticed the Teacher and some of his disciples also stood. This Jesus looked on the interruption, not with an air of superiority, as I would have expected, but with a mixture of compassion and—was that contempt?

One of the men wrestled the woman who clutched a cloth wrapped around her in an attempt to cover her nakedness. They forced her to stand before Jesus as the others gathered around. Upon seeing the Teacher she dropped her head.

Those in the back of the crowd stood.

"Teacher," one of the Pharisees said.

The courtyard silenced as everyone strained to witness this change of events. A religious leader near me fingered a rock. I now noticed many of the teachers and Pharisees had stones in their hands.

"Teacher, this woman was caught in the act of adultery."

The man called Jesus nodded. He looked at her, his brown eyes appeared compassionate rather than condemning.

"As you know, in the Law, Moses commanded us to stone such women. Now what do you say?"

Whispers slithered through the crowd. A man to my right leaned near me. "They are trying to trap him."

"Trap him?"

"Shush." People around me glared.

The man leaned in and whispered. "The religious leaders and Pharisees are jealous of him because the people consider him a prophet, maybe even the promised Messiah."

"Why would they be jealous? I would think they would be support-ing him. Haven't the Pharisees been telling us for years that the Messiah was coming?"

The man nodded. "It's one thing to envision a Messiah that will do what you want. It's completely another thing to have a Messiah who disapproves of what you do."

More strange words.

I noticed the woman hunched over, her face buried in her hands, trying to hide in the middle of this crowd with everyone looking on.

Her sins exposed for everyone to see. My own guilt in the old man's death rose to the surface and I swallowed.

I turned my attention to the Teacher. He looked at the group and the woman in particular and then bent down. "What's he doing?" I asked to no one in particular.

Whispers rippled to the back of the crowd. "He's writing something on the ground with his finger."

"We caught her in the act," said a teacher of the law.

With these words the woman let out a cry.

"Well, Teacher," said a Pharisee. "Are we to uphold the Law of Moses?"

Jesus stood and brushed the dirt from his hands.

The crowd quieted.

"If any of you is without sin," he said. "Then let the one without sin be the first to throw a stone at her."

The courtyard was silent and I felt a tension fill the air like wine expanding a wineskin.

Jesus again knelt and wrote on the ground.

An elderly teacher of the law slipped away from the group and left the courtyard. Next a white bearded Pharisee placed his stone on the ground and quietly walked away.

We all watched in utter amazement as one-by-one the woman's accusers walked away, first the older ones followed by the younger.

Now, only the woman remained. Jesus straightened and approached the woman, her body shook as she wept into her hands. The contempt I'd seen earlier was gone, departed with the religious leaders. Compassion was all I now saw on his face. "Woman, where are they? Has no one condemned you?"

The woman, scared and frail raised her face to him then slowly looked around to see her accusers had departed. Wide eyed, she shook her head. "No one, sir."

"Then neither do I condemn you," he said. His voice was sure yet kind, his face mild. "Go now, and leave your life of sin."

She stared at him momentarily then straightened, backed up several steps, turned and fled. As she passed I caught sight of her—head bent, hands pulling the cloth around her—attempting to block her face.

I watched her leave then looked back at this teacher they called Jesus. He did not condemn her. Why? Was she not caught in the act?

Does he not uphold the Law? How can he forgive her? Who is he to do such a thing?

Jesus resumed his teaching but I struggled to concentrate. I reflected on what had just transpired. She was obviously guilty and the Teacher never considered her otherwise. Yet, despite her sin, a sin requiring death, she left the temple court absolved. Her sin forgiven. How could that be possible? Shouldn't all sin be paid for?

An old familiar pang crept over me. I looked up at the Teacher and for a brief moment our eyes met. I shuddered. Those eyes. Those eyes. They were not the eyes of a stranger. A childhood memory appeared. No. How could it be? Despite the warm harvest weather a chill prickled my skin.

I closed my eyes and again saw those kind, brown eyes. The ache I'd carried since my youth argued with the emerging hope I felt.

Those who mourn will be comforted. The words from this morning crept into my mind. Was comfort possible?

CHAPTER TEN

TESTED

I struggled to reconcile this man speaking to the crowds here for the feast and the small child born in Bethlehem over thirty years ago. Did I dare entertain the hope that this was the same man? The Messiah? No, it couldn't be. All the boys his age were killed.

Boys. My boy. Where was Natan? I kept looking for him as I listened to the Teacher. The sun was high in the sky. I knew I should go look for my son, but this Jesus spoke with conviction and surety, not at all like the religious leaders.

It was strange for Natan not to come. I stood and skirted the edge of first the Women's court and then the other courts, but Natan was nowhere. Earlier my wife, Mary, and our soon to be married daughter had listened with me, but they left to prepare an afternoon meal.

Not finding Natan in the temple I left. The streets were full of people attending the feast. In every courtyard, rooftop, and open area people had erected booths to remember the journey our people took from Egypt to this land that Yahweh promised our forefathers.

I had just passed through the Valley Gate when a cart carrying cedar beams, escorted by several Roman guards, rumbled by. I stepped in behind the cart and searched for Natan. I hadn't gone far when a loud groan emanated from the cart ahead of me and I watched as the right wheel turned inward and broke away from the cart. Immediately the heavy load tumbled off.

People scattered to avoid the beams. Somewhere a child cried. The guards cursed their misfortune but soon turned to the crowd.

"You men, over there," a soldier shouted and grabbed one man by the arm. "Don't just stand there." He shoved the man toward the cart. "Get started cleaning up this mess." Several others followed in fear. "Each of you pick up a beam and start carrying it."

The men struggled to lift the heavy wood.

"Gaius," the guard called to a soldier near the oxen who had pulled the cart. "Show these men where to carry their loads."

Anger swelled within me. These Romans might rule over us, but not everyone in the empire was their slave.

All around, men slunk backwards hoping to avoid conscription into the Romans' free work force.

Why should we have to do their work? Didn't we have enough of our own? I too leaned away from the scene and had taken several steps back when I bumped into the metal body armor of a soldier.

"You, Jewish dog, get over there and carry one of those beams."

I turned and saw the older, but familiar face of Magnus, his javelin in one hand and shield in the other. The high afternoon sun glared off his helmet and shoulder plates. It had been ten years since he left Bethlehem and I had hoped to never see him again. But here he was.

He squinted at me. "A Jewish dog from Bethlehem. Welcome to Jerusalem. You're just in time to serve the Emperor." He pushed me in the direction of the broken cart.

I stumbled forward, wanting to scan the crowd for Natan but wise enough to know that such an action would be mistaken as resistance. I bent and grabbed a piece of wood, a sliver immediately punched its way into my finger. "What are these?" I asked another man also pulled from the crowd.

"Soon to be cross beams."

"For crucifixions?"

The man nodded, the beam on his shoulder.

I lifted the rough wood to my own shoulder and stepped forward. The beam was heavy and had obviously once been part of a home or workshop. I struggled to steady my feet as the road wound downward and then back up, alternating shoulders. My fury at the Romans fueled my body for the task.

Children stood at the opening of booths to watch the procession. I glanced at the hastily constructed shelters that were to remind us of our freedom from slavery in Egypt. How long would we endure these hardships until Yahweh sent a deliverer?

The meek are blessed, for they will inherit the earth. The words stumbled through my thoughts with every step I took. Was the Teacher mad? These Romans despised weakness. It was power and strength that they extolled—evident in their uniforms and variety of weapons. I failed to see how the meek could ever take over the earth.

With every building I passed, I knew I was going farther and farther from my wife and children—especially Natan. What right did these Romans have to force us to carry their heavy loads? Sweat trickled down my face. My parched tongue stretched to get even a few drops of the salty moisture. I tried not to think of the purpose this wood was destined for.

A man near the front of the line stumbled and fell.

"Get up," ordered a soldier. "We don't have all day."

For a moment we all stopped.

"What are you waiting for?" another soldier barked. "Keep walking." He poked the next man in line with his javelin, forcing him to step around the fallen man who struggled to rise and lift his beam.

We all followed.

Sweat soaked my garments and slivers worked their way through the cloth and into my shoulders. My hands stung from the bits of wood that pierced them.

As I reached the fallen man a soldier ordered him up and I glanced at the man still struggling, shocked to see he was a frail, old man. The soldier kicked him and yanked another man from among the onlookers to take his place.

We passed a well but the soldiers kept us moving forward. By now my wife would be wondering where I was. I thought of Natan and hoped he was safe and hadn't fallen into similar trouble.

The ground leveled somewhat and we struggled toward the upper city where the theater, Roman palaces, and towers were located. I transferred the beam to my other shoulder and heard a rip as my new tunic tore. New rage fueled me.

"How far are we going" I dared to ask the man ahead of me.

"Probably somewhere near the Gennath Gate."

I stumbled and almost fell. "The Gennath Gate?" A heavier wave of exhaustion fell over me followed by a deeper hatred for these senseless brutes. Leave it to a Roman to force bystanders to carry a heavy burden from one end of Jerusalem to the other.

My throat felt drier then I'd ever remembered. I heaved a sigh as the ground below my feet steepened.

"Get moving."

I felt a sharp pang in my back as Magnus shoved his javelin at me.

"This isn't lazy little Bethlehem, Uzziel."

I resisted the urge to swing the heavy beam around and hit him upside the head. The fact that I was shorter and would likely miss my mark was the main reason I refrained, though deep down I knew such an act meant certain death.

I saw anew the image of the woman caught in adultery this morning. By now it was mid-afternoon. I wondered what she was doing. How odd that our lives can take such quick turns—for better or worse.

CHAPTER ELEVEN

CAUGHT IN THE MIDDLE

I turned into a promising road, the buildings darkened with shadows. I walked a short distance until the street ended in a stone wall. In all my trips to Jerusalem I'd rarely entered the Upper City where Herod's palace and other government buildings were located. The landmarks were all unfamiliar as I meandered through dark alleys and streets lined with buildings boasting Roman architecture. I feared I'd wander until morning—my family worried.

"Excuse me." I stopped to ask a man standing near a booth where a woman cooked over a small fire. The smell of food filled my nostrils and taunted my hungry stomach. "Which way to the temple?"

He looked at my dirty skin and torn, bloodied tunic then back at me as though I were a beggar or thief.

"Please sir, I'm here—"

"That way." He pointed in the direction of the ever-darkening sky.

"Thank you."

He turned and entered his booth.

His wife purposefully busied herself with her cooking. I traveled east until I came to a well where I drank until the water sloshed about my stomach. I continued, often backtracking, as I worked my way to the lower city.

The last rays of light streaked across the tops of buildings as the roads finally became familiar—it wouldn't be long now.

I turned a corner to discover a group of men. "You there, why are you wandering the streets?"

My stomach clenched, agitating its liquid contents.

Within moments several men surrounded me. "I'm just returning to my lodging."

"Did I see you earlier today?" A young man with a long beard asked.

I shrugged. With so many people, how would I know?

"Yes." He nodded. "You spoke with Jesus Barabbas."

"What happened to you?" His companion asked, almost touching my garments.

"I was forced to carry a crucifix beam for some soldiers."

"Filthy Romans," the first man said and spit several times. "Go get the master," he told his companion.

Within moments Barabbas appeared. "Brother Uzziel." He kissed my cheeks. "What is this I hear the Romans forced you into labor?" He lifted the shoulder of my garment. I winced. "How did this happen?"

I told him and his men my story, my anger spilling forth.

"How many men were forced into this task?"

"Eighteen, twenty, possibly more."

"This is an outrage."

His men agreed with nods and words of assent.

Barabbas gripped my stiff and sore arm and turned me to look at several booths set up nearby. He waved his arms toward them and others seen on roofs. "Now is our time to move. While we are great in number."

My stomach constricted and the water inside jostled as if it were a wrung wineskin.

"Yes, now is the time," many of his men agreed.

"We'll purge this city and then our land of these foul swine."

All about me a chorus of voices joined in.

"Yes, yes."

"Purge it."

"Cleanse the land."

"Rid the land of the foul swine."

Right before my eyes all my dreams of childhood and early manhood rose to possible realization.

"Take advantage of our numbers," shouted another follower.

A family walked past, the husband eyed us and the wife hurried the children along.

"Reclaim the land of our inheritance."

Oh, freedom from the oppressive Romans with their swords, javelins, and daggers. An image of the burly Magnus and his fellow soldiers appeared as Barabbas' underfed men dressed in nothing more than cloaks gripped staffs or scooped up stones.

It was true, as a boy, King David had slain the giant Goliath. Although it was true, I was unconvinced of the sincerity of heart and dependence upon Yahweh this band of men possessed.

I considered the Teacher's look of compassion and true understanding I'd seen this morning. My host's words, *"Blessed are the meek. For they will inherit the earth,"* swirled around the growing agitation of Barabbas' men.

"Uzziel, what say you?"

I shuddered at Barabbas' words.

"Shall we attack tonight?"

For the first time in my life I faltered at the idea.

Several more groups of people passed us, the men stopped by several of Barabbas' men, attempting to draw them into the idea of revolt.

"No, no." An older man protested. "We want no part of this." His family watched from a short distance.

"You want no part of what?"

We all turned to see a large Roman soldier flanked by several others. The older man trembled. "I, uh, I, I want no part of—"

"This." One of Barabbas' men swung his staff at the soldier's uncovered knees. *Crack.*

Immediately there was a clash of bodies, armor, swords, rocks, shields, javelins, knives, fists, daggers, words, and screams.

"Papa." A small boy ran into the fray.

"Carmiel," the mother screamed.

My ever-stiffening muscles cringed as I saw a child, less than four years old, weave through the legs and weapons. His tiny body was jostled about. Amidst the grunts, thumps and clangs I heard his desperate voice, "Papa, papa."

I circled the group, which had grown in number and split, searching for the boy. A man tripped and stumbled backward, creating a momentary opening. I pushed my way in, elbows and fists jabbed my sore arms, chest, and back. A dagger grazed my cheek. I pushed others away with my hands, my vision focused on the ground and the pale cloth of the boy's garment.

I reached for him but he slipped from my hand. Carmiel. Was that the name his mother called him?

A rumbling sound filled the street. I looked up to see soldiers approaching from the direction I had come.

"Carmiel," I called. "Carmiel."

Around and above me people screamed warnings at the sight and sound of more soldiers.

"Carmiel." I saw him weave to my right and turned to catch him as a man collapsed near me and I had to jump to keep from stumbling over him.

The rumbling increased and I heard the howl of a child.

"No." I moved to where I thought I heard the sound but saw nothing. "Carmiel." A fist struck me in the jaw and I reeled back.

"Run, run." People on the rooftops yelled.

I rubbed my face. To my left I saw a narrow opening where I could escape. I pushed my way through the thinning fight to make my way there. That was when I saw the boy, crumpled on the cobblestones. I pushed a man, not caring who he was and ran to the child.

Blood pooled under the boy. The soldiers were only a house away. I scooped up the child.

"You there," a soldier yelled as Barabbas and his men fled along with bystanders.

I hurried to the narrow space between two buildings and slipped in sideways. In the street soldiers shouted and from somewhere I heard women crying. I pressed the small boy to my chest and listened for his breathing—the sound of my own labored breath and heartbeat filled my ears.

He lay so still in my arms, blood from somewhere on his head soaked into my tunic and ran down my hand. I felt with my fingers for the wound. Finding it I ripped a piece of cloth from my sleeve and pressed it to his head. I looked out to the street to see a soldier pass.

The child stirred and I almost shrieked for joy. I held him tighter and whispered soothing sounds. Small fingers clung to my beard.

In the street the sounds of fighting and soldiers quieted. People called to one another and I heard the grief-filled voice of a woman, "Carmiel. My son. Carmiel."

I wiggled my body out of the tight space, the rough stones scraping my back. A feeling I hadn't noticed in my flight.

"Oh, Carmiel. My son. What did they do with him?" The mother's voice rose to a shriek.

I emerged into the street and saw the mother kneeling on the ground near his lost cloak, searching for some sign of her son. She was flanked by her husband and family.

I approached, the boy now moving more in my arms.

"Mother, Mother," a girl about the age of Natan nudged the grieving woman, her eyes on me. "Mother, look."

At her words, they all looked up. The mother wailed. "Carmiel. My son. Does he live?"

The father stepped forward.

I held out the child. Carmiel moaned and lifted his head.

"My son." The father took him and in the torchlight of onlookers I could see streaks of blood, dirt, and tears on the boy's face. He stirred in his father's arms and whimpered as family gathered around.

My eyes met the father's and he opened his mouth to speak but words seemed to fail him.

I nodded.

Happy relatives pressed between us and after one more look I left.

Chapter Twelve

Unexpected News

"Uncle Roi, Uncle Roi," my son called as we arrived home in Bethlehem after the Feast of Tabernacles.

I bowed before my aging uncle and kissed his gnarled hands. After the death of my parents, the wise shepherd had assumed the position of family patriarch. "Blessings, Uncle Roi." I sat next to him. "We saw the Teacher, the one they call Jesus."

My uncle looked at me and I nodded. "Tell him, Natan."

Uncle Roi's grown daughter, Noy, brought water for us to wash our feet.

"He was there, Uncle. In the temple, teaching and debating with the Pharisees and other religious leaders."

"Natan, what did you learn?"

"He told us to love our neighbors. One of the religious leaders asked him who our neighbor was. So he told a story about a man traveling to Jericho who was attacked by robbers, beaten and left lying on the road. Both a priest and a Levite saw him but they both walked by. Then, guess who stopped to help him?"

"A shepherd?" Uncle Roi said, his lips spreading into a teasing grin.

"No, Uncle Roi. A Samaritan."

"A Samaritan?"

"Yes. He helped the man and took him to an inn and paid the innkeeper to continue caring for him."

"Well, isn't that a surprise?"

"Yes. The religious leaders thought so too. I don't think they liked that story."

"I imagine not."

"Father, can I go see my lamb?"

"Yes, Natan." I watched my son hurry out the door.

"So what do you think of this teacher?" my uncle asked.

I examined a cluster of grapes Noy had brought us. "I'm not sure what to think. He's not really what I expected."

"Is anything in life really what you expected?"

I chuckled. "No."

"I saw him save a woman caught in adultery from being stoned."

My uncle seemed to consider this.

"He is unafraid," I said.

"Unafraid of whom? The Romans?"

"The Romans, the religious leaders, anybody. He speaks his mind and he speaks with certainty and…and…" I searched for the right word, "…and power."

"As the Messiah should."

"Do you think this is the Messiah?" I asked.

"From the stories I've heard, yes, I do."

"But if he's the Messiah, why do the religious leaders seem at such odds with him? It's as though they keep trying to trap him."

My uncle leaned his sinewy body against the wall. "I have been pondering on the words of the prophet Isaiah." He took a sip of wine. "I believe Isaiah was speaking of the promised Messiah when he said, 'he was despised and rejected and we esteemed him not.' "

I bit into a grape and reflected on his words.

Uncle Roi laid his shaking hand on my arm. "I have wondered about these words many a time. But now, what you say you saw," he paused. "Well, maybe that is what the prophet meant."

"But what about the child born here thirty years ago? The one the angels said was the Savior?"

"What about him?"

"Well, how can this Jesus fellow be the Messiah when the Savior, the Christ, was killed?"

"Was he?"

I stared at my uncle. Had he gone mad? "Surely you remember the

Roman soldiers coming and murdering our—" I couldn't continue.

"Do you really think Yahweh would allow his Christ to be killed before he'd saved us?"

"You don't think he was killed?"

His countenance softened and he took on the expression of a child revealing a secret he'd eagerly desired to share. "I know he wasn't."

"How?"

"I saw them leave—the night before the soldiers came."

I stared at him. Questions formed then died on my lips.

"I was bringing a wounded lamb in from the fields when they passed by on the road. Though they were a stone's throw away I recognized them."

"Why didn't you tell me?"

"You never asked."

I pondered my uncle's story while he crushed grapes with his toothless gums.

Was it possible? I allowed the thought to take root. "Do you mean," I asked him. "That Joshua ben Joseph escaped Herod's attempt to kill him?" The realization filled my thoughts and excitement rose in my chest.

My aged uncle smiled.

"That means." I plucked a grape and worked it between my fingers. "He is the Messiah." Joy spilled into my heart. "But how did the carpenter know to leave the very night before Joshua would have been killed?"

My uncle shook his head at me. "After angels told us of his birth, you ask how Yahweh could protect him?" Uncle Roi leaned in, his face weathered but his smile quick and eyes bright. "The real question is, what will he do next?"

UNEXPECTED

OUTCOMES

CHAPTER THIRTEEN

PARADE OF PARADOX

"**F**ather, what is it?" Natan asked as we neared Jerusalem.

"I'm not sure."

Shouts rang up from a large throng of people winding down from the Mount of Olives and crossing the bridge over the Kidron Valley in the afternoon light.

"Can we go see?"

I paused, remembering my experience with crowds the last time I was in the city. The last thing I wanted was to have another confrontation with Magnus or any other Roman soldier for that matter.

A man approached carrying a load into the city.

"Sir, why the crowd?" I asked.

"The healer, Jesus, the one they call the Galilean is coming."

He continued on before I could ask any more questions.

"Did he say the Teacher was coming?" Natan asked, a wide grin on his face and a sparkle in his eyes. "Please Father, can we see him? I want to see him again."

I nodded and we walked north, Jerusalem's high walls on our left already casting shadows.

People drifted out of the city gates and were joined by others coming from Bethany. They all spoke of a man they said Jesus raised from the dead. "He is alive," said a nearby woman to another. "Lazarus is alive. The Teacher raised him from the dead. I wouldn't believe it had I not been there."

"So it is true?" asked another woman. "We have heard rumors."

"Oh, it is. He is among those hailing Jesus as our promised Messiah."

"We have also heard," added a man in the crowd, "that the religious leaders wish to kill Lazarus and this Jesus of Nazareth."

I shuddered at the thought. Why would they kill the Messiah whose arrival we'd waited for so long? I watched Natan to see if he'd heard this rumor, but he was too enthralled by the excitement building around us.

As we neared the group, we heard singing intermingled with shouts as the crowd moved about in celebration.

Some in the crowd waved palm branches. Occasionally I got a glimpse of Jesus.

"There he is," I pointed toward a knot of people for Natan to see.

Natan, almost as tall as I, stretched to see. "Oh, I see him," his voice cracked. "He's riding a donkey. It's the teacher we saw in the temple courts during the festival."

"That's him."

Shouts rang out as we walked toward the ever growing group of people.

"Hosanna." "Hosanna to the Son of David." The people cheered. "Blessed is he who comes in the name of the Lord."

I stopped in my tracks. Around me people flowed to join the procession.

"What are they doing?" Natan asked. "Why are they placing their cloaks on the ground? Look, his donkey is walking on their clothes."

An excitement swelled in my chest. "It is what we do when," I swallowed. "When we want to honor royalty."

"Father, they are waving palm branches and shouting 'Hosanna.' "

"Yes."

"Those reckless fools," a Pharisee near us exclaimed. "If the Romans see us waving palm branches they'll think we're planning to rebel like Judas Maccabeus."

A shudder ran down my spine. Was I ready for another confrontation with Roman soldiers? I watched the approaching procession. The Romans would surely see this as a sign of victory over them. I noticed Natan was deep in thought.

"Will the Teacher save us from the Romans like Judas Maccabeus saved Israel from the Seleucids?"

"I hope so." I took in the large crowd around him and couldn't stop the smile that stretched my lips. Freedom. The Messiah whom I'd seen as an infant had grown into the man, the king, who would save us from our oppressors. "Hosanna," I shouted. *Save us now*, my heart cried.

A dirty man passed before us. He waved a palm branch and danced about with the exuberance of a child. "That man," he said to no one in particular, "Jesus, Son of David, healed me." He turned to Natan and myself. "I was blind, but look, look." He pointed at his eyes. "Now I can see. I see trees and clouds. I see the fine weave of your cloak."

Natan looked at me, his own eyes wide with excitement. "When?" he asked the man.

"Today, son. Today."

"Father, did you hear him? Jesus healed." He pointed at the man. "He was blind. He sees now. He—"

My son seemed at a loss for words. Just then the group approached and once again I saw Joshua, now called Jesus, riding atop a young colt. His body gently swayed with the animal's movements. There was no arrogance on his face. No malice or contempt, like I'd seen in Herod and other Roman rulers.

Jesus looked at those around him with mercy, as though he understood our oppression and wanted nothing more than to lift the heavy burden upon us.

"Hosanna. Hosanna in the highest."

"Hosanna," I called and ran ahead. I pulled off my cloak, and laid it on the ground. Natan followed suit and we joined the crowd. Pride grew in my chest and spread to my extremities. For so long I had looked forward to this day and now, here it was.

The words of the prophet Zechariah came to me, *Rejoice greatly, O Daughter of Zion! Shout, Daughter of Jerusalem! See, your king comes to you, righteous and having salvation, gentle and riding on a donkey, on a colt, the foal of a donkey.*

"Hosanna to the Son of David," someone said.

A Pharisee near me called out to Jesus, "Teacher, rebuke your disciples."

The colt slowed and Jesus turned to the man. "I tell you, if they keep quiet, the stones will cry out."

The donkey stopped, Jesus sat erect and surveyed the great stone wall before him. People crowded around and we stepped back, but not before I saw his face moisten with tears. "If you, even you, had only known on this day what would bring you peace—"

Others crowded around me. "What's he saying?" "Shush." "I'm trying to hear."

"Father, can you hear him?"

I strained to hear but shook my head at him.

He moved forward and whispers filtered back.

"He said our enemies will build an embankment against Jerusalem."

"What?"

"When?"

"He'll protect us," some said.

The man who'd heard him continued. "We, our children, and the walls will be dashed to the ground."

"Oh, no. Say it isn't so." A woman covered her mouth.

"The Teacher said, 'They will not leave one stone on another, because we did not recognize the time of God's coming.'"

"What does he mean?" people asked.

Natan looked at me. I could only shrug my shoulders. His words and his ways always so unexpected. His words had little impact on the crowd.

I noticed most of his disciples didn't share the exuberance of the crowd. Instead, they looked rather concerned.

We entered the city with the throng. "Hosanna." "Peace in heaven and glory in the highest," shouted the people.

All around us people watched as the Teacher made his way to the Temple.

"Who is this?" those around the temple asked.

"This is Jesus, the prophet from Nazareth in Galilee," responded the crowd around us.

Many joined in the calls for salvation, but not the religious leaders. They scowled. Nearby a Roman centurion and his men watched, eyes alert, hands firm on their javelins, muscles taut.

CHAPTER FOURTEEN

FOOLING THE ROMANS

We approached the temple the following day to find vendors and money exchangers clustered on the streets, most in surly moods. As we entered the temple courts an odd calm and reverence greeted us.

"Uzziel, did you hear?" My cousin, Shai, approached with his three sons close at his heals.

"No, what?" I glanced around at the court. Where was everyone? Sure there were lots of people here for the Passover and the Feast of Unleavened Bread, but it wasn't as crowded as usual. Splintered wood lay scattered about and off to one side I thought I recognized a broken cage like the ones used to hold doves.

"The Galilean drove anyone who was buying and selling out of the temple," Shai said. "He knocked over their benches and overturned the tables of the money changers sending denarii and shekels everywhere." He moved his hands and arms about as if to recreate the scene for us.

"That explains the merchants in the streets and the calm in here," I said.

Shai's middle son held out his hand. "I even found two shekels."

Natan surveyed the courtyard floor.

"He wouldn't even let people carry merchandise through the temple courts," my cousin said.

"Jesus did that?"

"Yes."

"Why?" I asked Shai.

"He said, 'It is written, "My house will be called a house of prayer," but you are making it a den of robbers.' "

I raised an eyebrow. "My house?"

Shai nodded. "That's what the teachers and chief priests keep saying."

I looked about. There were no bleating lambs in pens and cooing caged doves. Gone were the cattle and the flies they attracted. I had to admit, the calm was nice. Occasionally an animal was led through the court to slaughter.

"He was certainly right about those scoundrels making it a den of robbers," I said. "Several years ago one of those merchants told me the lamb I'd brought was blemished and that I needed to purchase one of his for an exorbitant price. I would not be fooled with his deceit."

"And it's certainly easier to pray without all that haggling and commotion," Shai said.

The more I learned of Jesus the more I liked him. It looked as though he would not only rescue us from the Romans, but also from the corrupt religious leaders.

Six or seven children ran past us, some waving tattered palm branches, others strips of cloth. "Hosanna to the Son of David," they called.

Several religious leaders glared at them. "That Galilean will have the whole temple turned upside down if we don't stop him."

As two other children skipped past with palm branches, one of the Pharisees grabbed their little arms. "Stop this singing and nonsense. That man you celebrate is no Son of David."

The children nodded wide-eyed, and slunk off.

I shook my head. It was wrong for children to worship but permissible for merchants to steal?

"Come, let's go hear him," Shai said.

On our way to the inner court we walked by some Pharisees overseeing the cleaning of broken tables and cages. "First he comes in here and destroys the place," one said. "Then he tells us the prostitutes and tax collectors are entering Heaven ahead of us? By what authority does he say and do these things?"

"That man is out of his mind," the other said and lowered his voice.

"It's time we—"

As we passed them I could no longer hear what they were saying. But what was this claim that prostitutes and tax collectors are entering Heaven?

Prostitutes and tax collectors? I remembered the Feast of Tabernacles and the woman caught in adultery. The religious leaders were ready to stone her but Jesus stopped them. I remembered again the feeling of forgiveness she must have experienced—release from the prison of guilt.

We entered the inner temple court and joined the group already listening to Jesus. Some disciples of the Pharisees and several Herodians approached him.

I sat down, remembering the last time I'd heard Jesus speak.

"Teacher," the oldest in the group said. "We know that you are a man of truthfulness and that you teach the way of God in truth."

What kind of trap were they laying for him now?

The leader fingered the leather straps that held his phylactery to his arm. "You are not concerned about anyone's opinion, for you care not for a person's status. Tell us, then, what you think: is it lawful for us to pay the census tax to Caesar or not?"

I leaned forward, eager to hear his reply. His response could start a rebellion.

A quiet fell over the crowd. We were all tired of Rome's excessive taxes. Why should we support our enemies?

Jesus stood. "Why do you test me, you hypocrites? Show me the coin used to pay the tax?"

One of the men handed him a Roman denarius.

"Whose image is this? Whose inscription?" He asked.

"Caesar's," they said.

"Then give to Caesar what belongs to Caesar and to God what belongs to God."

Whispers, some of relief and others of displeasure rose from the crowd. Some in the crowd shook their heads in disappointment as the tension brought on by the question evaporated.

Those testing Jesus appeared amazed at his response. Unable to trap him they left.

I sat stunned. Give to Caesar what is Caesar's? How could he say that? None of this was Caesar's. We were God's chosen people. We did not belong to Caesar and neither did our money.

I stood as a group of Sadducees came to question Jesus. "Natan, I need to go out for a bit. Be sure to be at our host's home in time for supper."

"Yes, Father."

Shai glanced at me but I continued on and left the city through the Golden Gate. I really had no idea where I was going, I just needed to go somewhere quiet, alone.

"Yahweh, what are you doing?" I called to the sky as I climbed the Mount of Olives. "I do not understand." I entered a garden and sat below a tree. "Is this man the Chosen One, or not? If so, why does he waste time arguing with the religious leaders rather than confronting the Romans? Why does he tell us to pay taxes to Caesar? Why does he say that those who collect taxes for the Romans, over-charging us so they can profit, will enter Heaven above the religious leaders?"

I looked out over Jerusalem, my fingers gripping my outer cloak. "How can he forgive a woman caught in adultery and save her from the assault of her accusers' stones? What about your law? How can he raise a man to life after four days in the tomb?"

I snapped off a dead branch and broke it into small sticks. If he could do these things, surely he had the power as a child. "Am I any better or worse than they? If this is the Messiah whom I saw as a child in Bethlehem, why couldn't he have saved that old man from…?" I threw a stone at a tree. Would anything ever take away the secret guilt I buried every day?

For over thirty years I'd repressed my part in the old man's death. Now my body shook from years of regret, blame, and self-condemnation. Why after all this time did it rise to the surface? I tried to justify my actions, or lack thereof. I was just a boy. What if it had been Natan? Would I want him punished by the Romans? Age was of no consequence to them. They'd slaughtered all our infant boys. Crucifying a boy on the cusp of manhood would mean nothing to them. Just one less Hebrew to cause them trouble.

What if I were falsely accused right now? Would I want my family to suffer in poverty because I couldn't be there to care for them? Yet that is probably what happened to the old man's family.

As usual, it was a circular argument. And in the end, I returned to where I am—unable to change the past—condemned to haul it about.

I don't know how long I was there. The sun was high in the sky by the time I calmed myself. I washed in a nearby well and made my way back into the city.

Nearing my host's home, I stopped to buy some bitter herbs for the Passover meal. That's when one of Barabbas' men approached me.

"You were a friend of Barabbas, yes?"

I nodded, recognizing the man as one who was involved in the fight during the Feast of Tabernacles. "How is he?"

"You haven't heard about the master?"

"No. Is something wrong?"

"He's been arrested."

I paused. I was not fully surprised. It was bound to happen. "What are the charges?"

"Insurrection."

"Now what?"

"Rumors are they will crucify him."

Again the Romans win. I could no longer hope that Jesus Barabbas could save us. Jesus of Nazareth was our only hope. I just didn't understand his ways. Was his comment about paying Caesar what is owed a ruse to make the Romans think he wasn't a threat? I paused as the thought sunk in. A renewed energy filled my mind and body. Yes!

☙ ◆ ❧

That evening Shai and I tended to the Passover lamb he'd brought for the celebration.

I ran my fingers through the lamb's wool. "How do you think this Jesus of Nazareth will overthrow the Romans?"

"I don't know." He shrugged and gave the animal fresh water. "What makes you think he will?"

"Shai, that's why Yahweh sent him."

"From all I've seen he's more concerned about spiritual matters than politics."

"Ah, that's where he's got everyone fooled. I've been thinking about this."

"I'm sure you have. Can you hand me that rope?"

"He's planning to become king. Why else would he allow the crowds to welcome him into the city the way he did? Trust me, he plans to become king. But to catch the Romans off guard, he's making it look like he's only concerned about religious things."

"Oh. You're sure about this?" Shai closed the gate on the pen and settled under an olive tree.

"Of course I am. Jesus has this all planned out. You can't think it's just a coincidence that he was hailed as our King right before Passover?"

Shai said nothing.

"Cousin, you are so infuriating, just like when we were young boys. Don't you see any of this? Don't you care?"

"Of course I care. But I just don't think I see it the way you do. Don't you remember when the angels announced his birth to Uncle Roi and the other shepherds?"

"I was about to ask you the same thing."

"Well, there you have it."

"Have what?" I said, skipping a small stone across the courtyard floor.

"The angel's message. 'Glory to God in the highest heaven, and on earth peace to those on whom his favor rests.' "

"Yes, but sometimes peace must come with a fight."

"I've listened to him, Uzziel. He doesn't sound like that kind of fighter. The only ones he fights with are the hypocrites."

I chewed on a piece of st

. "I think you're wrong. You watch. He will free us from the Romans."

Shai stood. "Maybe."

I watched him leave. I knew I was right. I'd thought of little else the past two days. All over Jerusalem there was an excitement like none I'd ever felt during any Passover or any other festival for that matter.

With all the power Jesus possessed, who knew how he would do it? One thing I was sure about; when he did, it would be amazing.

CHAPTER FIFTEEN

CLASH OF POWERS

I awoke abruptly at daybreak the morning of Passover to my host's urgent words and his firm grip shaking me.

"Come, they have him. They've taken him to Pilate."

"Who?"

"The Teacher."

"Who has him?"

"The chief priests and the religious leaders. Word has it they arrested him last night."

I sat up and cinched my cloak about me.

"Father, what is it?"

"The Teacher, he's been arrested."

"No." Natan was up before I could say anything. "Why?"

"It is the jealousy of the chief priests and elders," said our host. "We must hurry."

"What can we do?" I asked and saw the same question in Natan's eyes.

Our host grabbed his staff. "Whatever we can."

My cousin and his sons joined us as we made our way through the streets of Jerusalem to the Praetorium, the governor's palace. Was this the Teacher's way of taking the battle to the Romans? Was he planning to perform some great miracle to overthrow our adversaries? Why else would he allow himself to be arrested and taken to the

Romans' seat of authority and power within the city?

The sun was well above the horizon when we reached the Praetorium. A large crowd was gathered outside, unwilling to enter. They feared entering Pontius Pilate's palace before the Passover and becoming unclean. In the shadows I thought I saw several of Barabbas' men. Soldiers stood at close intervals in case the throng chose to riot.

Our host looked around at those gathered. "I don't like this," he said.

"Why?" Shai and I asked.

"This mob is full of troublemakers."

I cringed.

The governor was nowhere to be seen. Some wondered if Pilate would release a prisoner as was his custom during the feast. How I hoped he would. I still wasn't sure if this was the Messiah's plan or if something had gone terribly wrong.

As we waited, some whispered that he would be released and others that he would be crucified.

My stomach clenched when I heard this.

Natan gripped my arm. "They can't kill him, can they?" Fear like I'd never seen paled my son's face. "What crime has he committed?"

"Where is the Teacher?" Our host asked those around us.

"He was taken to Herod," an older man said. "People say he returned just a short time ago."

"Herod?" I said to Shai, who just looked baffled.

An elder approached. "That man will only cause trouble for Israel," he warned us. "He has been stirring up dissent all over Galilee and Judea. If allowed to continue, the Romans will take away our state and temple."

We all looked at him, unable to believe his words. Was it possible?

"He must be crucified for the safety of all Israel. Better that one man die for all of us, than we all die."

Natan leaned into his cousin. "How can he say that?"

The elder looked directly at each of us. "We must protect our sovereignty."

A hush spread through the crowd as Pilate appeared and sat on his judge's seat.

We worked our way closer to the front as some within the crowd called for Jesus' release.

"He is guilty," some called.

"Crucify him," others said.

The hairs on my neck prickled.

Pilate raised his hand to restore order.

The crowd settled.

"You brought me this man as one who is inciting the people to rebellion." The governor glanced at the growing crowd but focused on the religious leaders. "I have examined him in your presence and have found no basis for your charges against him."

"He should die," a man yelled.

Pilate glared at the elders after the insolent interruption. "Neither has Herod, for he sent him back to us. As you can see, he has done nothing deserving of death. I will punish him and then release him."

As with one voice, the chief priests and elders cried, "Away with this man!"

Pilate shifted in his chair, a stern look of frustration on his face.

Several in the crowd jeered.

"Crucify him! Crucify him!" others called.

My heart pounded in my chest. "Why?" I said to no one in particular.

"I don't know," Shai muttered.

Natan turned to me. "What are they saying? Can't they see that Pilate doesn't fear him?"

I looked at my son, who in spite of his age, was fighting to hold back tears.

All around us people shifted and whispered. The braver and more foolish called out.

Pilate again calmed the crowd. "It is your custom for me to release to you one prisoner of your choosing at the time of the Feast."

"Release a prisoner," many in the crowd shouted.

Hope grew in my heart. Yes, the custom. I thought of the crowds who had hailed him as king only a week ago. Surely they would rally for his release. Then, in his time, he would free us.

"Which do you want me to release to you: Barabbas or Jesus, called the Christ?"

A lump rose in my chest. Barabbas? I had given him money to carry on his work against the Romans. How many times had we talked? I believed in his cause. It was my cause too.

Natan looked at me. He'd heard me speak of Jesus Barabbas and his efforts to free our people.

Now, it was either the Galilean or Barabbas. Sights and sounds swirled around me. A dull throb pulsed at my temple. It was one or the other.

"Barabbas!" someone shouted.

"Barabbas!"

A man near me called out, "Jesus!" and I wondered which prisoner he meant.

Religious leaders worked their way through the crowd. "Barabbas!" they said. "Barabbas!"

People who'd been quiet or yelled for the Christ now called for Barabbas' release.

Were they afraid? I'd heard the rumors. People thrown out of the temple for following the Messiah—ostracized from neighbors and friends, their businesses shunned.

"Father," Natan looked to me. "Barabbas has killed people." He swiped at a tear. "But the Teacher—"

I nodded. Natan was young and his judgment unclouded. Still, I struggled. I had hoped if one couldn't save us the other could. Barabbas was more aggressive but Jesus was God's Messiah with supernatural power and a large following.

Pilate's voice rang out above the crowd. "Do you want me to release the king of the Jews?"

"Yes," Natan said. His voice cracking as he spoke.

"No," shouted the rulers. "Not him! Give us Barabbas!"

"Jesus, the Messiah," Natan's voice was bolder now. Several others joined him.

All around us shouts for Barabbas rang out.

Natan's expression grew more worried but also determined. "The Teacher! Give us the Teacher!"

A scribe standing near me glared. "Get your son under control."

I tried to respond, but words wouldn't form.

"Barabbas," the crowd called.

"The Teacher!" Natan's voice was louder still.

"Your son." The scribe scowled.

My son? My son? I looked toward the judging seat. "Jesus of Nazareth," I shouted. Faint at first, then louder.

All around us people shouted, "Barabbas! Give us Barabbas!"

Pilate commanded our attention. "Then what shall I do with Jesus called Messiah?"

"Crucify him," said the elders and leaders.

"Why? What crime has he committed?"

"Crucify him!" They shouted louder and louder. People jostled one another.

I shook, unable to believe what I saw and heard. Sweat ran down my temples. My vision blurred.

Pilate stared at the throng. The soldiers positioned near him and around the courtyard stood vigilant, spears in hand.

"Crucify him!" someone shouted.

Again Pilate spoke. "Why? What crime has this man committed? I have found in him no grounds for the death penalty. Therefore I will have him punished and then released." He motioned to a guard who left.

The chief priests and religious leaders pressed the crowd to crucify Jesus.

Pilate got up and left.

My host shook his head. "I can't believe it has come to this."

"You knew this would happen?" Shai asked.

I leaned in to hear his answer.

"They have been threatening to kill him for quite some time."

"I thought those were only threats," Shai said.

The sun continued to climb in the sky as we mulled around. Hunger, anger, fear, and the prodding of the religious leaders set our nerves and emotions to boiling.

Pilate returned and the noise dulled. "Look, I'm bringing him out to you that you may know I find no basis for a charge against him." Pilate stretched out his hand.

A large soldier came, his red robe bustling behind him. Beside him, firm in the soldier's grip was Jesus, the Christ.

"Here is the man." Pilate said.

I gasped at the sight of him as did others around me. Amongst the religious leaders and their disciples angry shouts rang out. "Crucify! Crucify!"

There, not thirty feet away stood Yeshua—who they called—Jesus. He was bloody and beaten from the whipping he'd received. A purple robe, saturated in blood, hung from his shoulders, clinging to the exposed flesh from the many gashes on his arms, legs, chest, and back.

"Crucify!"

Natan stared, his lower lip firm between his teeth. He turned to me. "Father. Why is there a ring—" He gulped. "Of thorns pressed into his head?"

A sob rose in my chest followed by anger. "They mock our Messiah, our king."

"Crucify! Crucify!" the elders shouted some more.

"I find no basis for a charge against him," Pilate repeated.

"We have a law," the chief priests said. "And according to our law he must die because he claimed to be the Son of God."

At this, Pilate stood, his face pale. He looked first at the leaders and then at our beaten Messiah. He left for the palace and motioned the soldier with Jesus to follow.

When Pilate returned the religious leaders continued to shout their demands. "If you let this man go, you are no friend of Caesar's." "Anyone who claims to be a king opposes Caesar."

All around us the intensity increased.

"I'm afraid there's going to be a riot," my host said.

"Crucify him! Crucify him!"

My hands shook. "No. No," my voice absorbed in the cacophony of voices around me. "Give us Jesus," I shouted louder. How could they do this? It was wrong. All wrong.

"Crucify him!"

Anger swelled within me. "No," I shouted at the top of my voice. "No." I turned to those around me. "Can't you see what they're doing? He's innocent." I shook several men near me. "He's innocent. Can't you see that? He's innocent." They shoved me away.

"Uzziel," my host grabbed me. "Enough. You can't stop this."

All around me men shouted, "Take him away." "Crucify him."

I wrestled myself free. "I will. I will stop this. I have to. He is our Messiah. I can't let them do this." I pushed my way closer to the front. "Stop. You can't do this." I pulled at a Pharisee. "You can't do this." I reached my free hand to Jesus. "He is the hope of Israel."

The Pharisee pushed me away. "Get your hands off me."

"No." I flailed and someone kicked me.

"Take him away," the leaders chanted. "Take him away. Crucify him!"

I panted, trying to catch my breath.

"Shall I crucify your king?" Pilate asked.

"We have no king but Caesar," declared the chief priests.

I ran my hands through my hair and pulled at my beard. This couldn't be happening.

Pilate shook his head. He called for a pitcher and washed his hands. "I'm innocent of this man's blood," he said. "It's your responsibility."

"His blood is on us and on our children," shouted the people.

Natan made his way to me. "Father, how can they do this? Tell me his blood is not on us."

I pulled Natan to me and we wept. He was so young. Too young, Yahweh. This is not what I wanted for him. To bear the shedding of innocent blood. It was too heavy a burden. Once again I had failed.

Cheers rose around us. I looked up to see Jesus Barabbas led from the Praetorium. He raised his fists in the air like a hero as people shouted his name.

I turned from him and spit. "Let's go."

The man who told me Barabbas had been imprisoned approached. "I can't believe my eyes. Barabbas is free. Can you believe it?"

I looked back at my former savior and walked on.

My host returned to his home. Shai and his sons left also.

CHAPTER SIXTEEN

HOPE SLAIN

Natan and I followed the procession, as Jesus carried the heavy cross through the streets of Jerusalem. People clustered to see this spectacle—the man who was to become their king now trudging to his death. Between the crowds of people I caught a glimpse of our Messiah, so beaten. Every step—a struggle. I remembered the pain and thirst, the dehydration and exhaustion I'd felt carrying that cross beam.

Why hadn't Jesus done something? Hadn't he just raised a man from the dead several days ago? I thought about all the miracles I'd been told about. This made no sense.

When he faltered and could not get up, the soldiers commandeered a man from the crowd to carry the cross to Golgotha. I remember very little of that procession. My thoughts were filled with the trial. There must have been some way I could have changed the outcome stopped this murder. But I was helpless.

I climbed the hill to the place of the skull. The crowd fanned out. Two other prisoners were also there, stretched upon their crosses.

Nearby a Roman centurion barked orders. His voice sent shivers across my skin. The centurion turned—it was Magnus. Hatred swelled within me at the sight of him.

Callously, as if he were tearing down a wall, Magnus commanded his men to drive long, thick nails through our Messiah's wrists and feet into the rough wood. There was no empathy or compassion—just another job.

Magnus gave another order and his men lifted the cross and dropped it into a hole in the hard, stone ground. I cringed as Jesus' body jounced, his weight pulling against the nails in his wrists. Blood pulsed from his wounds and he cried out in agony. I thought of the sharp splinters against his raw flesh.

"Why God? Why?" I whispered. "Wasn't this the One you promised would save us? Why is he hanging on that accursed cross and not one of these Romans?"

The chief priests and elders stood off by themselves. One of them called out, "He saved others but he can't save himself."

Several chuckled.

"If he's the King of Israel, let him come down from the cross right now and we'll believe him."

I looked at Jesus. He had healed the blind and even raised some from the dead. Yet he was silent.

"He trusts in God. Let God rescue him, if he wants him," the man jeered.

"He did say, 'I am the Son of God,' " said another religious leader.

"Father, why are they saying those things?" Anger and confusion intertwined in Natan's voice.

My chest tightened. "I don't know."

Flies buzzed about us and crawled upon the flesh and open wounds of those hanging on the crosses. At first they moved their heads like a horse or donkey might to remove the pests. But eventually they seemed to give up. Above us, ravens, hawks, and other carrion eaters circled and swooped. Their very presence chilled my flesh.

I watched as the man I'd seen teach and forgive hung helpless. He looked with grief on those who insulted and mocked him. He said nothing. To think I had held his hands as a small child, caught him when he jumped from a tree. A wineskin full of sadness, confusion, regret, and anger welled up inside me and poured from my eyes. I turned away and covered my face. "No. No. Lord, how can this be?"

"Don't the priests and elders know he's the Messiah?" Natan asked.

I could only shake my head as I glared at them. Why were they killing our Messiah? For years they'd told us the promised Messiah was coming. Now that he was here they taunted and killed him? Did they like Roman rule?

"Father?" Tears streamed down Natan's face.

I pulled my son into an embrace.

"Are they jealous?"

"Maybe. I don't know." I wiped more tears from my face. "I don't understand any of this. This is not the way it was supposed to be."

The crowd behind us pushed us forward until we were near the soldiers. There were four of them including Magnus, who was in charge. Once again he was shedding innocent blood. How did this man live with himself? How did I live with myself?

As the condemned looked on, the four soldiers sorted through first one criminal's clothes and then the other's, each taking some. When they got to Jesus' clothes they divided his garments into four shares.

"How about this piece?" One of the soldiers held up a seamless undergarment.

"That's of good quality. Let's not tear it."

"I agree."

Magnus joined the small group and inspected the finely woven material. "Let's decide by lots who will get it."

I watched in disgust as the soldiers squatted right in front of Jesus and cast lots to see who would win his garment.

Natan scrunched his face. "Do they have no honor?"

Behind me a group of travelers stopped. "Look, isn't that the man who healed people?"

"The healer? Cursed by God and hanging on a tree? How could he be our Messiah?"

"What's his charge?" asked another traveler.

Several men stepped past us. " 'This is Jesus, The King of the Jews,' " said one, reading the sign Pilate had nailed above him.

"Ha, doesn't look like any king I've ever seen."

They shook their heads.

"Hey, Jesus, King of the Jews," one of them called. "You said you would destroy the temple and rebuild it in three days."

"Doesn't look like he's going to accomplish that," someone muttered.

"Unless he plans to rule from on that cross."

"Come down and save yourself."

"If you're the Son of God," another added.

Several of the soldiers sat as they watched the criminals struggle to breathe.

All around me religious leaders, soldiers, and others mocked and insulted the man the angels had told my uncle would save us. I watched as Jesus looked upon us. Though I wanted to lash out at them all, I didn't. His expression stopped me. There was no anger or hate. In his eyes, I saw sadness. Not for himself, but—for us.

Then, one of the criminals called to Jesus. "Aren't you the Messiah? Save yourself and us."

Jesus just looked at the man as if the thief was lost and confused.

"Come on, Messiah." The thief paused to lift his body and take a labored breath. "You made people walk."

"Don't you fear God?" asked the man on the other cross. He let his weight drop to the nails in his feet and grimaced at the pain. "We are getting what our deeds deserve." He coughed and struggled to raise his body. "But this man." He took in a jagged breath. "This man has done nothing wrong." The criminal's body lowered onto the nails in his feet and he again pushed his body up to take a breath then turned to the Teacher. "Jesus, remember me when you come into your kingdom."

Jesus inhaled deeply and looked at the man with the same compassion I'd seen when he'd forgiven the woman caught in adultery. "I tell you the truth, today you will be with me in paradise."

"Be with him in Paradise. Ha!" said a man next to me. "He can't even rescue himself from the cross."

Suddenly the sky darkened and we all looked to see the sun directly above us completely covered by dark clouds. A chill settled upon us. Whispers and murmurs spread throughout the crowd. Natan cinched his outer garment about him and examined the sky. "Father, the birds are gone."

I looked. He was right, not even a sparrow fluttered about.

"I think it's a sign from Elohim," he said.

I gazed up at the man I thought would save us. Just a week ago he entered Jerusalem as a king and now he hung dying like a criminal— unwilling to save himself. Why? I thought he would save us. But watching him I realized I didn't understand him at all. Why didn't he climb down from that cross and send both Romans and mockers running?

Occasionally someone would shout at him and others would laugh.

Behind the crowd of men, I saw a group of women watching. Probably some of his followers.

Natan searched the sky, trying to determine the time. "Father, we've been here for at least four or five hours."

"I know."

Something about Jesus drew my attention to him. He seemed to be gathering his strength. His head was down, his body hanging from the nails inside his wrists. I watched as he pressed against his feet and lifted his body—taking a breath as he did.

"Eli, Eli, lema sabachthani."

"He's calling Elijah. He's calling Elijah," the people behind us said.

Natan perked up. "Do you think Elijah will come?"

"He's not calling Elijah."

A man worked his way through the crowd and lifted a sponge filled with wine vinegar upon a staff up to Jesus' lips.

"Now leave him alone," someone shouted.

"Let's see if Elijah comes to save him."

"If he's not calling Elijah," Natan said. "Then what did he say?"

"My God." I paused in my translation. Tears welled in my eyes. "My God, why have you forsaken me?" My shoulders convulsed. Why God? Why *did* you forsake him?

The crowd waited. First in silence, but when nothing happened people shuffled, some left, travelers on the road stopped to gawk. More people passed by and shouted, "Hail, King of the Jews."

One of the soldiers shouted up at Jesus, "If you're the King of the Jews, save yourself."

I glanced at Magnus. He stood, solemn.

Some in the crowd jeered.

I sensed Natan's increased agitation.

"Elohim's not sending Elijah, is he?"

I shook my head.

"I can't watch this any longer. I can't watch as the hope of Israel dies."

I looked at my son, on the cusp of manhood. He was older than I when I met the Messiah. He fully knew the implications of the Messiah's coming and also his death. Our hope for freedom from Roman occupation hung on that crude tree.

Another religious leader mocked Jesus and I found my hatred for them grow alongside my hatred of Rome.

"I understand, Son. Why don't you return to our host's home."

Natan looked again at the bloodied man on the cross. "Aren't you coming Father?"

I swallowed, my throat dry. How could I think of my own thirst while our Messiah suffered. "No. I'm staying."

"But, Father—"

"I first saw him when he was just a few hours old. I held him, entertained him when he was a small child so his mother could cook and clean."

Natan cocked his head. "You? What? I don't understand. Why didn't you ever tell me?"

"What was there to tell? I thought I'd lost him when the Romans killed all our little boys."

"Then why does Yahweh allow them to kill him now?"

I shook my head. "I don't understand any of this. But what I do know is that I can't lose him."

"But he's dying." Natan looked first at Jesus then up at the dark sky and rubbed his arms. It was noticeably colder.

I stared up at my Messiah. "I must stay with him."

"I want to go to the temple and pray."

"You may go." I looked back at Jesus only to find him watching me. For several moments we just gazed at each other.

There was a rustling behind me and Jesus lifted his eyes. I turned to see a man and several older women make their way through the crowd. One of the women appeared familiar.

"Is that one of his disciples?" someone whispered.

"I don't know?"

"I think it is," said another.

"Look. His mother." A woman near me said.

"That's his mother," others whispered the news to those around them.

I looked at the women and tried to determine which one was Jesus' mother. Back then Mary had been so young, a smile spread across her face as she held her newborn son. Then I recognized her, standing near the disciple. She was older, with grief carved into her once soft skin.

"Woman," Jesus spoke, his voice gentle but raspy.

She looked at him with anticipation.

"Here is your son," he said, his head tilted to the man by her side. Mary looked to the disciple and wrapped her fingers around his arm. Jesus addressed the man standing there. "Here is your mother." He nodded and placed his arm around her.

"I'm thirsty," he cried.

A sponge was lifted to his lips.

"Father, forgive them for they do not know what they are doing."

My body shook and I fell to my knees. "Yahweh, no. Please don't let this happen." I watched Jesus labor to take another breath.

Jesus lifted his gaze to the sky. "Into your hands I commit my spirit."

With those words his head slumped and his body hung limp.

My chest felt cracked like an egg and all my hopes, hurts, and fears spilled out. All was silent and then it felt as though someone shook me. I turned to see who it was. That's when I saw trees sway and Jerusalem's wall shudder. The crash of several buildings as they crumbled inside the city. People grabbed at each other and several shrieked. The crosses swayed.

Mary cried and covered her mouth.

Some in the crowd struck their fists against their chests. Whether in sorrow, woe, or anger I wasn't sure. Maybe all.

The crowd thinned. I just knelt there—unable to rise. A movement to my left caught my attention. I watched as Magnus approached the cross and stood just in front of me.

He plunged the blunt end of his spear into the ground. "Surely this was the Son of God."

My fingers scraped at the stone and packed earth. I lifted my hands above my head and allowed the dirt to fall onto my head and shoulders. I rent my tunic.

By now it was mid afternoon. A Pharisee approached Magnus and asked that the criminals' legs be broken as the law commanded that no body should be left hanging overnight. The soldiers broke the legs of one criminal and then the other. But as Jesus was already dead, one of the soldiers pierced Jesus side with his spear. Immediately blood and water flowed from the wound.

I took one last look at the Christ and left.

CHAPTER SEVENTEEN

BITTER HERBS

I returned to my host's home, my heart heavy and hardly in the mood to celebrate the Passover. While I had been away, Shai had taken the lamb to the temple to be slaughtered.

It was nearly twilight when I arrived at the house. My host gave me the basin with the animal's blood. As the sun set and the first stars brightened in the soft blue sky, I took hyssop and spread the lamb's life blood upon the door posts and across the lintel above his home. The blood spilled onto my hands and the smell intensified the day's events in my mind.

We then roasted the lamb over the fire.

In hushed tones, Shai told me of the earthquake and how the large, thick curtain separating the Holy of Holies ripped from top to bottom. I thought back to Magnus' words, "Surely this was the Son of God."

I stared at Shai, trying to take in his words. What could this possibly mean? Was this a judgment against the religious leaders? Against us?

"It's frightening," Shai whispered. "To think that we could walk straight into the presence of God."

I pondered his words as I performed the ceremonial washing. We then reclined about the table on cushions. In Egypt, our forefathers had eaten the first Passover wearing sandals, their garments tucked into their belts, and staffs in hand—prepared to leave. Today, I just wanted to leave.

Our host stood at the head of the table. "The story of Passover is a story of our deliverance from bondage and each element of the meal is a picture of our redemption."

"What is the meaning of the greens?" we asked.

"The greens represent life," he said with leafy greens pinched between his fingers.

"What is the meaning of the salt water?"

"The salt water is the tears of life. Before we eat the greens, we dip them into the salt water, for truly…"

"…a life unredeemed is a life immersed in tears," we replied.

With that, we dipped the greens into the bowl of salt water. Tears fell from the leaves upon the table and plates as we brought them to our lips.

I glanced at Natan who sat next to me. He was becoming a man and participated as one, his countenance serious and attentive to all that was said. Was he trying to push the day's events from his mind?

"What is the meaning of the root of the bitter herb?" we asked.

Our host held up the root. "We are reminded by this root that life is often bitter. So it was for the sons of Israel," he paused, "in the land of Egypt."

So it was even now, I mused.

"What is the meaning of the bitter herb itself?" everyone asked.

In unison we fathers spoke, "As we partake of the herb, we are reminded again of how bitter life is without redemption."

I saw my grief reflected in Natan's eyes.

We each ate of the bitter herb on pieces of plain, flat matzah. The sharp, spicy flavor of the bitter herb filled my sinuses. The small child sitting across from me scrunched his face and tugged on his mother's sleeve.

"What is the meaning of the Passover lamb?" we asked.

"The Passover lamb reminds us of the lambs slaughtered at twilight in Egypt and their blood that was placed over the doors and on the door posts of the homes," replied the fathers. "That the angel of death would pass over the houses of the children of Israel in Egypt, when he smote the Egyptians, and delivered our houses."

Outside I heard the tramp of soldiers' feet as they patrolled the empty streets. The taste of bitter herbs still fresh on my tongue.

"But why the blood upon the door posts?" asked a child.

"It is the blood of sacrifices that atone for our sins and redeems us from death, as the law declares," said our host.

We all responded, "Blessed be Yahweh who redeems us."

We then sang a song.

"We have eaten the bitter herb and have heard of the Passover lamb, but what about the unleavened bread?" we asked.

Our host held up a piece of matzah. "The bread of affliction which our ancestors ate in the land of Egypt."

Several of the smaller children squirmed.

"What is the meaning of the unleavened bread?" we asked.

"It is the bread of affliction that we may remember the day our ancestors left the land of Egypt. For in a hurried flight they left the land of Egypt."

"But why no leaven?" asked a different child.

"As a small piece of leavened bread is used to ferment an entire batch of dough that it may rise," we fathers answered. "So a small amount of sin spreads throughout our lives and causes our own desires and self importance to rise in our own minds that we disobey Yahweh."

"We eat the unleavened bread to show Yahweh our devotion to live lives dedicated to Him," our host reminded us. "We will eat no leaven tonight or for the following seven days."

He then lifted a stack of three matzahs, each separated with a cloth and removed the middle piece of unleavened bread. He broke the middle piece in two, setting one piece aside while wrapping the other in a piece of white cloth. "You children must close your eyes as Uzziel here hides the piece wrapped in cloth."

I took the broken matzah and slipped from the table hiding it in an empty clay jar and placed the lid atop it.

As I returned to my seat our host continued speaking to the children. "We must buy it back from the child who finds it, or the Passover cannot be concluded. And remember…"

"…great is the reward of the one who finds the hidden matzah," we said.

The Passover continued with the children asking questions and our host explaining how our ancestor Joseph was sold as a slave into Egypt by his brothers. "God raised Joseph to a position just under Pharaoh." Then, during a mighty famine, Joseph was reunited with his family and they were invited to live in Egypt."

"They began as only eighty, but after four hundred years the Israelites grew in number and might with large flocks. A Pharaoh, who did not know of Joseph feared the numerous Israelites and forced them into cruel labor. When the Israelites cried to Yahweh for help, he sent Moses as our deliverer."

As our host told of God's judgment upon Egypt through the ten plagues I thought of how many times I had cried out for deliverance. I squeezed back a tear.

Our host was now at the tenth and greatest plague, when the angel of death killed the firstborn of every home without the blood of the lamb painted on their doorposts.

"And this is why we celebrate the Passover," he said.

The roasted lamb was set on the table. The smell of the seasoned meat filled the room.

"In one house shall it be eaten," we said together. "Neither shall you break a bone of it. Neither shall any meat be left until morning."

"Let us eat the lamb," our host said.

Though I hadn't eaten all day I struggled to partake of the meal. Just yesterday I had marveled at the anticipation I felt toward this year's Passover. It was as though I were truly among my ancestors. Never had I felt the immediacy as I had with this Passover. Our Messiah had been hailed as king. It had seemed only a matter of time before he would rescue us from the oppression of Rome. But Rome had killed him—at the insistence of our own leaders.

A tear slid down my cheek and fell onto the lamb before me. How truly bitter was an unredeemed life.

CHAPTER EIGHTEEN

SURPRISED AGAIN

The following day was the Sabbath and we rested, though my mind was busy trying to make sense of the recent events. On the first day of the week Natan and I rose early and said our goodbyes.

"You won't be staying for the rest of the Feast?" our host asked.

"No."

He placed a firm hand on my shoulder, reminding me of my father. "These have been hard days. I understand, my son."

Natan and I walked back to Bethlehem in silence.

At home we were greeted by my wife and older sons and their children. "Home so soon? Is everything well?" She looked at Natan, his expression sullen.

"May I tend to the sheep?" he asked.

"Yes."

Mary touched my arm. "What is wrong?"

"They killed the Teacher?"

"The Messiah?"

I nodded.

"Lord save us."

I wrapped my arms around her.

"Uzziel, is that you?" Roi called.

"Yes. Uncle."

I kissed her then went to see the aging shepherd.

"Surely the Feast is not over yet?"

"No, Uncle Roi. I just could not stay."

He patted the cushion next to his mat. "You seem very upset, what happened?"

I sat down and told him about the week's events. He listened intently, his eyes still as bright as when he was young.

"There is so much I don't understand. Why did our own leaders have Jesus killed? And Pilate, why did he want to free him? What about God's plan? How was Jesus' death part of God's plan? I was certain Jesus would save us from the Romans."

Uncle Roi sighed. "Many very good questions. Most of which I can't claim to know the answers to." Then his eyes twinkled. "But your questions remind me of a conversation I once had with Joseph when Jesus was still a baby."

I leaned in.

"Joseph once told me that when he was engaged to Mary, but before they were married, she was discovered to be with child."

I drew back. "Really?" I remembered the woman at the temple caught in adultery.

My uncle nodded. "Joseph was grieved, he didn't understand. He loved her very much and couldn't possibly bring himself to have her stoned to death. So he was going to divorce her quietly."

I could already imagine the sense of rejection and hurt Joseph must have felt. Confusion and disappointment rose in my mind. "Are you saying Jesus wasn't the Messiah after all?"

"No, not at all."

"Then what are you saying?"

"Listen," Roi said. "One night, after Joseph had decided to divorce Mary, an angel appeared to him and told him to take Mary as his wife."

"What?"

My uncle held up his bony hand. "Now listen to this. The angel told Joseph the baby inside Mary was conceived of the Holy Spirit."

"Conceived of the Holy Spirit?" I cocked my head. "You must have misunderstood him."

"No." Roi placed a hand on my arm. "There's more. Something I've always wondered about. Something I've pondered on for many years. Something I know even Joseph wondered about."

I leaned in even closer.

"According to Joseph, the angel said they were to give the child the name, Joshua—"

"Jesus in Greek."

"Which means the Lord saves," Roi said. "But that's not the interesting part."

I raised my eyebrows.

"They were to name him this because he would save his people from their sins."

"Their sins?"

"*Our* sins."

I pondered my uncle's words. How could he save us from our sins?

"Don't you see?" continued my uncle. "This Messiah that Yahweh has sent us was not born in a way that we expected. He did not live or do things as we expected. He didn't come for the reasons we anticipated his coming. So why should he die like we would expect?"

"Uncle Roi, you're only complicating this."

He chuckled.

I started to speak then stopped.

He watched me. His crazy sheepherder's grin spread across his sun-etched face. "Think, Uzziel. You know the Scriptures. 'Therefore the Lord himself will give you a sign: The virgin will be with child and will give birth to a son, and...' "

" '...will call him Immanuel.' " I stood, thinking of the things he had said and done. "They killed him because he claimed to be God."

"I do not know all the answers. God's ways are above our ways. We must trust him. You must allow the Lord to comfort you. As our father David said, 'The Lord is close to the brokenhearted and saves those who are crushed in spirit.' "

I nodded. Those crushed in spirit. That would describe both my son and I. "I should go see how Natan is doing." I stood and made for the door when the rest of King David's words came to mind. " 'A righteous man may have many troubles, but the Lord delivers him from them all; he protects all his bones, not one of them—' " I paused. " '—will be broken.' "

"What is that?" Roi asked.

"Not one of his bones will be broken."

Now it was my uncle's turn to look confused.

"The rest of King David's words: 'Not one of his bones will be broken.' The soldiers, they broke the bones of each of the criminals crucified with Jesus. But they didn't break his."

Uncle Roi considered this.

"But I'm still not sure what it means."

Shouts, talking, and the sound of sandals slapping the hard dirt echoed outside the house. Within moments the door burst open and Shai's sons poured in, followed by their father.

"Cousin Uzziel, Cousin Uzziel, you're not going to believe it. Where is Natan?"

"Here I am." Natan slipped in the door behind them. "Why all the shouting?"

The boys fidgeted with their desire to share the news but kept quiet as their father spoke.

"Uzziel. You left Jerusalem too soon." My cousin wrapped his hands around each of my arms and pulled me into him, patted my back, and kissed each of my cheeks. Shai's face was radiant. "Shalom. Hosanna. The Teacher is alive."

I shook my head. "No, Shai. He is dead. I saw it. I watched him die. I saw the blood and water spill from his side. This is no way to greet me."

"But it is true." He looked at his sons. "Isn't it boys?"

They nodded.

"Jesus is alive."

Uncle Roi and I looked at Shai and the boys. "What do you mean?"

"He has risen from the dead," Shai said.

"How? When?"

"This morning. Some women went to the tomb to anoint his body for burial. The stone was rolled away and his body was gone. An angel said he had risen, just as he said."

Natan's eyes were wide and shining.

"Everyone in Jerusalem is talking of it. Some of his disciples also went to the tomb and found it empty. Others have seen him. People say before he died, he prophesied that he would rise again in three days."

"What does this mean?"

"I don't know. But everyone is filled with joy. Well, almost everyone."

I felt dizzy and leaned against a wall. What had I once heard? It was about John the Baptist. "Shai, do you remember what I told you about that man they called, John the Baptist?"

Shai thought. "Vaguely. Did it have to do with calling Jesus a lamb?"

"Yes. The Lamb of God. That was it. He called Jesus the Lamb of God, who takes away the sins of the world."

"See," Uncle Roi said. "What did I tell you? The angel told Joseph that Jesus would save us from our sins."

"Surely that is it." I started pacing around the room. "Yes. That's it. The Passover lamb. No broken bones. The shedding of blood to atone for sins. Our sins. Redemption from death."

I grabbed my cousin by the shoulders and shook him. "Redemption. A life unredeemed is a life immersed in tears. He wants to redeem us. To save us not from the Romans or even the religious hypocrites. He says he is close to the broken hearted. He wants to wipe our tears away."

Our wives and other neighbors now filled the room. "Did you hear? Did you hear?" I kissed Mary on the lips. "He is alive. The Messiah is alive." I swung my granddaughter into my arms and patted a neighbor on the back. "Jesus is the Lord. And if he can forgive a woman caught in adultery—if he can ask God to forgive those who mocked and killed him..." I paused. Was it possible? I thought of how Jesus had looked at me just moments before his death. I thought of the old man who died because of me. I thought of all my hatred toward the Romans and every other sin I'd committed.

"Grandfather, why are you crying?" my little granddaughter asked.

I hugged her. "Because, finally, for the first time in my life, I am free."

PROPHECIES IN ANTICIPATED

The below noted Bible texts refer to Old Testament Prophecies, either quoted or referred to in *Anticipated*. Note that these are just a few of the 300 plus prophecies about Christ. I've also included a few New Testament Prophecies I felt were applicable.

Chapter 1
- Stars as signs for sacred times – Gen 1:14
- The people of Israel would be as numerous as the stars, refers to God's promise to Abram – Genesis 15:4-5
- "The people walking in darkness have seen a great light—" Isaiah 9:2 (NIV)
- References to Migdal Eder – Micah 4:8 (It is believed by many Jewish scholars that the promised king would be revealed at Migdal Eder, the tower of the flock, which served as a place to birth temple lambs and watch over the lambs destined for sacrifice.)

Chapter 2
- The Messiah was to be born in Bethlehem – Micah 5:2 (NASB)
- References to Migdal Eder – Micah 4:8 (see comments above)

Chapter 3
- The Messiah was to be born in Bethlehem – Micah 5:2 (NASB)
- The new star revealing Israel's great king – Numbers 24:17-19

Chapter 6
- The Messiah was to be born in Bethlehem – Micah 5:2 (NASB)
- The new star revealing Israel's great king – Numbers 24:17-19

Chapter 7
- Rachael mourning for her children who are no more. A reference to the murder of boys 2 years and older in Bethlehem – Jeremiah 31:15

Chapter 12
- Jesus would be despised and rejected – Isaiah 53:3

Chapter 13
- Israel's king comes riding on a donkey, the foal of a donkey – Zechariah 9:9
- Christ's prophecy of the destruction of Jerusalem which was fulfilled in 70 A.D. – Luke 19:41-44

Chapter 14
- God's house will be called a house of prayer – Isaiah 56:7

Chapter 15
- Jesus did not fight his arrest or conviction – Isaiah 53:7
- To be hung on a tree or pole meant you were cursed by God – Deuteronomy 21:23
- He was pierced for our transgressions – Isaiah 53:5
- They looked upon him whom they had pierced – Zechariah 12:10

Chapter 16
- The captivity of the Hebrews for 400 years was foretold to Abram – Genesis 15:13-16
- The bones of the Passover Lamb are not to be broken – Exodus 12:46, Numbers 9:12

Chapter 17
- The virgin birth and name to be Immanuel – Isaiah 7:14
- "The Lord is close to the brokenhearted and saves those who are crushed in spirit." – Psalms 34:18
- A righteous man's bones will not be broken – Psalms 34:19-20
- The bones of the Passover Lamb are not to be broken – Exodus 12:46, Numbers 9:12
- Christ's Crucifixion including his pierced hands and feet, and the casting of lots for his clothes – Psalms 22:16-18, Isaiah 53:4-7
- They looked upon him whom they had pierced – Zechariah 12:10
- Jesus' words that he would rise from the dead – Matthew 16:21, Luke 18:31-33, John 12:23-28
- Jesus' promise to raise the temple—his body – John 2:19, Matthew 26:21
- Prophecies that he would rise from the dead – Psalms 16:10
- Jesus the Lamb of God – John 1:29

DISCUSSION QUESTIONS

1. Could you relate to Uzziel? Why or why not?

2. Uzziel wants desperately to defeat the Romans, but when he finds himself face-to-face with Roman Soldiers he shirks. Why do you think that is? Have you ever been in a similar situation?

3. Why do you think Uzziel expects the promised Messiah to rescue his people from the Romans?

4. Why do you think Jesus didn't save the Jews from the Romans?

5. Why do you think the religious leaders didn't recognize their promised Messiah? Why do you think they demanded his crucifixion?

6. In the story it seemed that evil often won out over good. Does that seem true to life? What have you anticipated that didn't occur the way you expected? Can you see good that occurred as a result of things not turning out as you anticipated?

7. Throughout the story, Uzziel desires freedom from Roman oppression. In the end, what does he find freedom from?

8. How did the theme of guilt appear throughout the story? Were there other themes you noticed? What were they? How did those themes weave themselves through the story?

9. How do the events of the story relate to us today?

Ida Smith

ACKNOWLEDGMENTS

A special thanks to all my friends and family who have encouraged me along the way. To my husband, Rick Smith, for reading and editing draft after draft. To Taun Allman, for coming to my rescue with your artistic talent, when all my cover ideas failed. To Misty Clark and Pastor James Green for your feedback. Thank you to all my readers who enjoy my stories and share them with others. And of course, thank you to my friend and savior, Jesus, who invites each of us into His story.

About the Author

IDA SMITH grew up listening to stories of her parent's adventures in the wilds of north Idaho and Alaska. She started her first story when she was nine. Ida enjoys exploring new places and has visited Belgium, France, the Netherlands, China, Canada, and Mexico—besides much of the United States. Ida loves researching interesting facts about locations and history for her stories.

Find out more and Sign up for the *Jagged Journeys'* Newsletter and receive short stories from Ida Smith in your inbox at IdaSmithBooks.com

Also by the Author: *The Invisible Cipher*

NEIL GATLIN'S BAD CHOICES AND WORSE LUCK ONLY MULTIPLY—EVEN WHEN HE TRIES TO MAKE GOOD.

Used to failure, Neil is on the verge of fatherhood and desperately wants to succeed. Instead, his bad choices trap him between both sides of the law. As Neil flees from police he stumbles upon a murder and must choose between doing right or escaping.

Soon his life is in a downward spiral into greater danger than even he thought possible. Now he's in a fight for his life trying to decipher clues to the hidden truth before others' lies and deception entangle him—for good.

WHAT READERS ARE SAYING ABOUT *THE INVISIBLE CIPHER*

*"The Invisible Cipher: A Jagged Journeys' Novella, is a touching tale about a young man who really wants to live a normal, trouble-free life, but danger just seems to follow him. The story has light Christian undertones that are significant to the action-filled plot, with a few Bible scriptures used as examples in certain scenes. Numerous twists made **The Invisible Cipher** an even more interesting and suspenseful story. The situation that Neil found himself in could happen to anyone, giving the story a realistic feel. Ida Smith writes very descriptively and did a great job creating this lovely story."*
—**Michelle Stanley** for Readers' Favorite